Charles Hallock, Clarence Hawkes, Elbridge Kingsley

Pebbles and Shells

verses

Charles Hallock, Clarence Hawkes, Elbridge Kingsley

Pebbles and Shells
verses

ISBN/EAN: 9783337387167

Printed in Europe, USA, Canada, Australia, Japan

Cover: Foto ©Andreas Hilbeck / pixelio.de

More available books at **www.hansebooks.com**

PEBBLES AND SHELLS

VERSES

BY

CLARENCE HAWKES

WITH ILLUSTRATIONS BY ELBRIDGE KINGSLEY

PICTURESQUE PUBLISHING CO.

NORTHAMPTON, MASS.

1895

THE BRYANT PRINTING COMPANY,
FLORENCE, MASS.

DEDICATED

To my mother who first inspired me to write, and has since
been my constant helper.

INTRODUCTION

"Ye who love the haunts of Nature,
Love the sunshine and the meadow,
Love the shadow of the forest,
Love the wind among the branches,
And the rain shower and the snow storm,
And the rushing of green rivers,
Through their palisades and pine trees,
And the thunder in the mountains,
Whose innumerable echoes
Flap like eagles in their eyries : Listen !"
                                        —*Longfellow.*

In accordance with the above adjuration, so captivating to those to whom the apostrophe is addressed the almoner who subscribes himself herewith, at once opens out this new and effervescing volume of poems for their perusal, bespeaking from the world of letters a sympathetic ear, and consonance with its song : for,

The Book of Nature is ever full of ecstasy and beauty. Its leaves turn toward the sun. Its music is eolean. Its fountains are pellucid and inexhaustible. From its sources we have to draw and drink refreshingly. Perchance some of those who read these stanzas — some of those who have trod the sylvan paths which Thoreau so much loved, and which Longfellow never tired of describing with his pen, may be persuaded to link arms with the blind author, and so all saunter on together?

It has been well said that there are but few great Nature lovers ; that is strictly speaking, whose souls are in attune with the Creator's : but there have been a sufficient few to stamp their personality on the regions which they have animated. Thoreau's country, simple as it is, plain in its features, rough in its contour sometimes, is lovable because Thoreau has been there. We love the sods and the brown leaves which his feet have pressed. The wildwood precincts are hallowed by his memories. Men die, voices fail, and sentiment decays. Catbirds which are melodious in June squawk in August. Nevertheless, we love them all, birds and human kind, for what they were, and for what they have made their little spots of earth ; and so, when the Hadley poet sings, we love him too. A quiet bit of country under an observant eye can be made to yield a store of happiness. Dudley Warner wheeled his settee around the garden-oak, to follow the sunshine or the shade, until he wore a path in the grass. N. P. Willis wrote winsome letters from under a bridge. And now, herewith, a vista opens before us down the forest lane. Methinks I hear the muffled drum beat of a partridge in the spruce. "Listen!" We feel already an impulse to proceed. Come with the poet ! He will not sing in vain.

Our favorite Eugene Field is wont to dwell with sentimental fondness upon the memories of his dear Hampshire Hills : the old homestead, the cow pasture, the yearling colt, the watering trough, the deserted mill, the little red school house, and the playmates of his youth. But his reveries are liable to start a tear or draw his readers off into overgrown lanes and solitary corners, while Hawkes' themes, which bubble and flow from the self-same hillsides, are for the most part sparkling, treating of the ecstasies of the present hour. Sun pictures they are, indeed, and all the brighter, apparently, for being physiologically developed in the dark ! He says himself :

> "'Tis not for wealth I sing my simple lays,
> Or e'en for fame, or for the critic's praise,
> But for the joy of feeling and of living
> All that I say, and for the joy of giving."

The outburst is spontaneous and continuous. Perhaps it is because he is so young? And so we find his treble keyed to the notes of the bluebird. He twines his lute with the flowers that bloom in the spring and the clematis which climbs up over the porch. In the sunny corner he weaves his webs of fancy, while he inhales the sweet aroma which lures the insect tribes. In his mind's eye he watches them, as they flit from anther to corolla, and following after, gathers poesy from each bloom. Forsooth, it is a blessed thing to have no eyes, and so shut out the hideous things of earth !

Na'theless, the mind will not permit the material senses to dwell always in Elysium. Whenever the imagination strays into the Valley of the Dark Shadow, as it must sometimes, it conjures up all sorts of sombre themes ; and on such occasions the vagrant muse emits an undertone like the rumble of water in a deep cavern. It is then the poet writes dramatically of battle fields and carnage in which he has had no part, and of chimeras which he has never seen. Ah ! this discerning with the spiritual eye ! who shall fathom it ? Biologists are puzzled. But are not these mysterious lucubrations which so much surprise us, really the outcome of the divine nature which is in man ? scintillations of omniscience, as it were, which we are told is an attribute of the immortal world ? Does Drummond inform us exactly where the natural and the spiritual meet and blend?

It was my good fortune to be domiciled during the summer of 1893 under the same venerable rooftree with my blind young friend whose all seeing Muse has inspired this book of poems. I have touched elbows with him while we strolled under the spreading elms which double line the main thoroughfare of historic Hadley, and marvelled as we walked, to discover that his perception was in some respects more acute than mine; especially on pitch-dark nights, when I had to depend upon his subtle acumen to avoid obstacles which my natural eye could not perceive! He says the air seems more dense when objects intervene. And so it is that he recognizes open spaces and solid ·bodies like houses, trees and telegraph poles, as he passes along; or persons as they approach, on foot or in vehicles, even at considerable distances. He has correct ideas of locality and associated landmarks, and an apprehension of dangerous proximities, seldom stumbling over obstacles, or into a hole. In fact, throughout his everyday life there is a constant manifestation of psychical phenomena which it will be useless to attempt to account for until we come to realize that the carnal envelope with its five so-called senses is actually a hindrance rather than a help to a free operation of the spiritual energy.

In the case of Clarence Hawkes, he seems to possess the gift of clairvoyance. He easily discovers articles mislaid; reads character with correctness by a grasp of the hand; and when introduced to strangers will size up their height, weight, features, age, and state of health, as soon as he shakes hands with them. He knows when chairs and tables are removed from their wonted places without having to ascertain by feeling for them, and he can tell when people are in the room and how many there are even when perfect silence is preserved. No meteorological changes escape his notice. Fair weather cheers him and dull weather depresses him, more than it does most of those who see. He identifies the birds by their chirps and carols, the flowers by their odors, shrubs by their leaves, trees by their bark, and fishes by their shape and fins. He is a critical musician and a piano tuner, plays chess, works a type-writer, keeps scores of ball games, and travels all over the country without a companion. Few habitues of the mountain streams which thread his native hills in western Massachusetts are more deft in casting a fly or worm, or handling a trout. Most remarkable of all, he has discovered that the gamut is prismatic and that sounds have color. Middle C, he says, is deep red, and each ascending note grows lighter by degrees until the highest becomes white ; while the lower tones are graded in darker shades till the very lowest shows black.

Mr. Hawkes received a four years' course of instruction at the Perkins Institute in Boston. His study of elocution at that time has fitted him for the lecture platform which he adorns. He has also been a successful magazine writer. His poem "Erosion" took the fourth prize among two thousand competitors for the prizes offered by the Magazine of Poetry this year. His younger brother, it is due to say, has been his constant help as reader and amanuensis for several years.

It is half a century since the literary world possessed a blind poet. Percival of New Haven was the last. But Percival had not the refined intellectuality of the author of this volume. As yet it is too soon to define his position among the literati ; but if "Pebbles and Shells" are an index, the Blind Poet of New England is destined to occupy a high place among the great bards of America. The merits of some part of its contents have been so signal as to elicit an autograph letter of approval from Hon. Robert T. Lincoln, ex-Secretary of the Navy.

CHARLES HALLOCK.

CONTENTS

ILLUSTRATIONS

Eight Engravings directly from Nature by Elbridge Kingsley.

The Blind Poet at Work.   "The Mountain to the Pine."   "In the Wood."   Lookout Mountain.   "Sunshine and Shadow."   "Where There's a Pond with Lily Pads."   "The Deserted Homestead."   "The City of the Dead."

INTRODUCTION ....   BIOGRAPHICAL SKETCH............

POEMS OF NATURE

POEMS OF WAR AND PATRIOTISM

POEMS OF LOVE

POEMS OF CHILDHOOD

POEMS OF OLD NEW ENGLAND

MISCELLANEOUS POEMS

BIOGRAPHICAL SKETCH

FROM THE MAGAZINE OF POETRY

Clarence Hawkes, better known as the "Blind Poet of New England," was born in Goshen, Mass., December 16th, 1869. When nine years of age, he met with an accident while returning from school, which culminated in the amputation of one leg. When thirteen years of age while out hunting he was accidentally shot by his companion and both eyes were injured.

After undergoing several severe operations in hopes of regaining his sight, this hope was abandoned and at the age of fifteen he entered the Perkins Institution for the Blind. Here in addition to the regular course, he studied music and piano tuning, and was graduated after four years, taking the last two years' work in one. The following year he returned to the school for a post-graduate course, and at the same time began the study of law and oratory with teachers from Boston Colleges. After six months of arduous study his health gave way beneath the strain and he returned home to his parents, then located at Cummington, Mass.

One year was then spent in recruiting, and at the age of twenty-one Mr. Hawkes went upon the platform as a pnblic lecturer, and at the same time began writing short stories and poems for local newspapers. Since that time he has written three hundred poems and over fifty short stories and sketches, and lectured in nearly all parts of New England.   He is at present a contributor to over a score of the high class periodicals. Mr. Hawkes travels alone on his lecture trips and gets about with the greatest ease.   He is a base-ball and football enthusiast, a skillful fisherman and an accomplished chess player, while one of his chief amusements is to visit a picture gallery.

POEMS OF NATURE

IN THE WOOD

On woody mount, in mossy dell,
Who hath not felt that magic spell
   That steals o'er heart and brain, .
A sweet delight that ebbs and flows
As freely as the zephyr blows,
   Or falls the summer rain.

How well I know its every mood —
That gentle spirit of the wood!
   That bids all sorrow cease;
A subtle something in the air
That softly steals away all care,
   And fills the soul with peace.

It lives and breathes in every flower,
It whispers in the leafy bower
   Where drowsy insects drone;
It rises into sweetest swells
Where the sequestered veery dwells
   And chants his love alone.

It bursts into a mighty roar
When winter sweeps the forest hoar
   With howling hurricane;
It murmurs low in brooklet flood,
And smiles in every bursting bud
   When spring comes back again.

When autumn lights her crimson flame
What artist would not give his fame
  To paint so rich and rare?
When winter robes the firs in white,
Resplendent in the morning light
 What jewels tremble there!

How soft the wind of summer eves
That gently whispers in the leaves
  Of lordly forest trees?
How wild the whirling tempest's breath
That wails the dirge of summer's death
  In magic minor keys!

Ah, Nature! wrap thy dreamy shade
About the life that thou hast made,
  And let me slumber long!
Thine echoes softly, sweetly roll
Through hidden chambers of the soul,
  And teach the poet song.

WHERE DWELLS THE SPIRIT OF POESY?

Where dwells the gentle soul of poesy?
Upon the cloudy rifts of the rainbow skies,
Deep hidden in some maiden's love-lit eyes,
Or at the bottom of the rolling sea,
Far down in sunless caves of mystery?

Or doth her voice in sweetest accents rise,
From bird, or brook, or is it in the cries
The wild wind wakes upon the lonely lea?

The soul of poesy is everywhere,
Unto the eyes and ears of him who sings,
And all the world is filled with wondrous things,
To him whose soul reflects the beauties there.—
There is no thing so mean the worlds among,
That is not mete to grace the poet's song.

THE DESERT

Boundless, changeless, and cruel as the sea,
With brazen skies and suffocating air,
With burning rocks and sand, and blinding glare,
And silent ether, heavy with despair,
Stretching away e'en to infinity.

DAWN

Slowly the waning stars above grow dim,
　　Flicker and pale, like sparks that disappear;—
Far in the east, the cold horizon's rim
　　Softens a shade as dawn of day draws near.

Then comes a flush, a soft, pale crimson streak,
　　That warms and mellows as the young day
　　　　grows

Until it burneth like a maiden's cheek,
   Or deeper like the crimson of the rose.

But higher still the day's avenging fire
Streams o'er the ramparts of the flying night,
Flooding the world with swift effulgent light,
   Waking a thousand songs from Nature's lyre; ·
And then the great sun rolls his golden car
   Up from the east and drives the night afar.

TWILIGHT

After the sun goes down into the west
   And day's last glowing embers slowly die,
   And fades the glory of the sunset sky,
There comes an hour of all the day the best,
The twilight hour, when cares are laid to rest;
   Then o'er the fields deep cooling shadows lie;
   No restless zephyr stirs the sleeping rye,
And all the little birds have sought their nest.

Softly the night comes creeping o'er the land,
   Folding the earth in cool refreshing shade,
   Moistening each thirsty flower and leaf and
      blade,
With gentle dew, distilled by heaven's hand;
   So swift it comes, that, e'er they drink their fill,
   The calm night reigns on field, and wood and
      hill.

THE GLACIER

Softly sliding, slipping slowly down,
Each moment farther from the mountain's crown
The glacier comes;— and so the human will
That retrogrades, each hour gets lower still,
Until at last, beside the mountain's base
We scarce can recognize the old-time face.

ELEGY AT THE BIRTHPLACE OF BRYANT

Like pilgrims to the shrine we climbed the hill
  To view the spot where Nature's bard was
    born,
To get perhaps a momentary thrill
  From "classic ground," or from the summer
    morn.

It was the month when earth and heaven vie,
  Of balmy air, and tender bursting buds,
Above the deep cerulean of the sky,
  Below, the verdure of the fields and woods.

We heard the south wind stir the half-grown corn,
  The babbling of a brooklet fleeing fast;
And low of kine upon the breezes borne,
  And song of birds, that caroled as we passed;

We saw the vastness of the cloudless dome,
  The endless beauty of the verdant earth;
And on a distant hill, the summer home,
  And at our feet, the scene of Bryant's birth.

But now no dwelling crowns the cellar wall,
 For, long ago, its beams and rafters fell —
Only a marble shaft, not broad or tall,
 Amid the solitude stands sentinel.

And now, no children's merry shout is heard,
 That sound of yore that cheered the poet's
  heart
Yet still there comes the "lilting" of a bird,
 And one wild rose has not forgot the spot.

There is no trace of footsteps on the lawn,
 No vestige of the well-worn gravel path, —
Even the rustic gate and fence are gone,
 So time obliterates the scars of earth.

And he, the noblest of that happy throng,
 That gaily gathered here in years of yore,
The fair, the brave, the high-souled, and the
  strong,
 Is gone, and earth shall see his face no more.

Only the sweep of deep eternal hills,
 Frescoes of earth, against the dreamy sky,
The reverent soul with awe and rapture fills,
 Unchanged since when it cheered the poet's
  eye.

And can it be that all which he has said,
 The works of years, will fade away like this?

That, one by one, the burning lines will fade,
   Until the eye discerns but emptiness?

Ah, no! 'twas not with blocks of wood he
     wrought,
But with the hard-hewn rocks of solid truth,
Building them high into the temple, Thought,
   Where they are mortared in eternal youth.

And they shall stand, until the human heart
   To Nature's simple song no longer thrills,
Years after men forget this quiet spot,
   Far up amid the dreamy Hampshire hills.

GOD'S MIRACLES

Why talk of wondrous miracles of yore,
When June comes whisp'ring at thy lattice
door,—
Are not the springing grass and op'ning flowers
God's miracles through all the summer hours?

GREAT AND SMALL

The grain of dust that dances in the sun
Obeys that law that guides the heavenly
spheres,
And all the stellar bodies, one by one,
Go swinging round, obedient to the years.

ENVIRONMENT

A wondrous shell was thrown up from the deep,
Where it had lain long centuries asleep —
But, in a day, the sunlight and the dew
Had cracked and stained this shell of wondrous
hue.

MY AVIARY

My aviary is the deep green wood,—
I would not cage its songsters if I could.
Sweeter the song of one wild bird to me
Than all the notes of sad captivity.

THE HURRICANE

The azure sky grows green like ocean's brine,
The listless air is hot and strangely still,
And yet there comes a momentary thrill,
As of the coming storm, to give a sign;
The lowering clouds have gathered into line,
Their dark array enfolds the distant hill,
And on the air, so suddenly grown chill,
There comes the moaning of the rocking pine;
Then clouds of leaves and dust sweep down the
      lane,
Close followed by the howling hurricane.

Swift forked lightnings twist their snake-like
      forms
Among the clouds, and fill the sky with dread;
Deep throated thunders bellow overhead
And all things bow before the King of Storms.

SONG OF THE BROOK

I come from afar up the mountain,
   The favorite child of the snow;
I leap from a laughing wee fountain,
   And fall in a basin below.

By churning and boiling and gushing,
   I pierce through a dark mountain wall,
And into the sunlight come rushing,
   To fling far a beautiful fall.

Now down a long stairway for giants,
  From basin to basin I spring;
All foaming, and roaring defiance,
  My spray to the breezes I fling.

Then into a peaceful green meadow
  I lazily, placidly flow,
And thence to the woodlands' dark shadow
  With laughter and dancing I go.

I sparkle and bubble with pleasure,
  As over the pebbles I slide;
I murmur a musical measure
  As under the willows I glide.

In springtime I water the flowers
  That nod their sweet faces to me;
In summer I drink up the showers,
  And hurry them off to the sea.

When Autumn's rich beauties are dying —
  Then sadly I murmur my lay;
When o'er me the snow bank is lying,
  I gurgle the winter away.

I ripple, I dimple, I bubble —
  I chatter by day and by night. —
My laughter will banish your trouble,
  My song is a giver's delight.

Don't stop me to idle or dally,
  My life-work is ever to flow;
The meadow, the mill-wheel and valley,
  Are waiting to greet me below.

I pause not in lakelet or river,
  I rest not in woodland or lea,
Still onward and onward forever
  I flow to the boundless blue sea.

INFINITY

I took swift wings, that knew no time no space,
  And fled unto the utmost star that shines,—
  E'en to the end of things, that man divines,
Yet cannot see, then turned my eager face
To view the sight — to find some resting place
  For human faith — a revelation grand;
  But saw the countless stars on every hand
That lit great planets in their endless race.

Again I sought a star remote and dim
That flickered on the far horizon's rim,
  But saw the same deep, star-bespangled blue;
Yet once again I fled for countless years
Through endless deserts of unnumbered spheres,
  But with each hour the stellar pageant grew.

THE HANGBIRD'S NEST

Fashioned so fair, this small inverted dome,
With bits of moss, and grass, and strings,
And underneath the brooding wings,
Four tender, tiny, gaping things,
And near the nest the one who sings.
Ah! heart of mine, is this not truly home?

'TIS MARCH

'Tis March and far o'er hill and dale,
With rush, and roar, the winter gale
    Through bitter cold is flying;
While down beneath the frozen snow,
The fairest flowers that ever blow
    In winter graves are lying.

No sunshine melts the icy hand,
That still in grip-like iron band
    The tend'rest life is holding,
Unwarmed by any parting light,
The dreary mantle of the night
    About the earth is folding.

Nay! fret thee not — the day will come
When from their far-off sunny home,
    Will come the Southern breezes,
To melt away the ice and snow,
And whisper to the flowers below —
    " Dread March no longer freezes."

Then birds will sing in all the bowers,
And softest clouds and fairest flowers
  Will whisper joys unspoken;
All Nature'll sing a sweeter song,
Because the winter has been long,
  And now his chains are broken.

'Tis March, and o'er my weary soul
Misfortune's storm with ceaseless roll,
  Its onward march is sweeping;
While far beneath the lapse of years
Long buried there, with many tears,
  My fondest hopes are sleeping.

No sunshine ushers in the day,
No sunbeams fall across the way
  To cheer a heart that's weary;
And still the darkest storm-clouds lie
Across the azure of my sky,
  And all is dark and dreary.

Be strong, my heart! I know some day
That all thy clouds shall roll away,
  By fortune's breezes driven;
'Then hope shall scatter all thy fears;
A sunny smile shall dry thy tears,
  And thou shalt see but heaven.

THE BLUEBIRD

Fair herald of the coming spring
  That fearest not the winter's snow,
  The friendly fields begin to show,
O haste thy gaily-painted wing
I long to hear thee carolling
  Upon the tree-top, sweet and low;
  For when I hear thy song, I know
That soon the robin too will sing,
And all the merry woods will ring
  With Springtime's well remembered song;
  That flowers will wake from slumber long
And lift their fragrant offering —
Didst know what joy thy song would bring,
Dear little harbinger of spring?

THE MAYFLOWER

A beautiful floweret was sleeping
  Down deep 'neath the grasses and snow;
The chains of the winter were keeping
  Its color and fragrance below.

But springtime, with softest of breezes,
  With laughing and smiling all day,
Soon shamed the dark season that freezes,
  And melted the snowdrops away.

Then down came a cold April shower,
And dashing the floweret with spray,
It parted the folds of her bower,
And showed her the light of the day.

Oh, sweetly then smiled the fair sleeper,
And op'ning her eyes to the light,
Her beauties grew wider and deeper,
The smile on her face grew more bright.

Our sorrows are falling like snowflakes,
Our pleasures are melting like snow;
Kind nature ne'er thinks of our heart-aches;
A flower is sleeping below.

She melts us with showers of trouble,
(For life hath its seasons of rain);
Our tears are the fouutains that bubble
In deserts of sorrow and pain.

She rouses the soul that is sleeping
With showers so chilling and cold;
New treasures she gives to its keeping;
The beautiful petals unfold.

THE CLIFF AND THE SEA

Like some imperial fortress dark and lone,
With frowning walls, the cliff o'erhung the sea;
And little waves caressed it tenderly,
Yet each advance was coldly backward thrown,

Then angry grew the sea, and on the stone
   Heaped mighty waves that struck with thun-
     derous shock —
   Yet all in vain they beat upon the rock
And wind and wave subsided with a moan.

Then spake the sea in deep and sullen roar
   That echoed far along the rocky strand,
Behold! My waves shall break upon this shore,
   And I will lash the cold repellant land,
Until this cliff that proudly towers me o'er,
   Beneath my feet shall be but grains of sand.

PEBBLES AND SHELLS

THE PHEBE

Calling its plaintive note from post and tree
  The Phebe comes, nor has he other range;
And this poor song is like a life to me
  That moves in one dull round, and cannot
  change.

THE PITCHER PLANT

With parted petals to receive the dew,
And sun and rain this flower in beauty grew;
And so must we unfold onr hearts to hold
The sun and shower of wisdom manifold.

THE RAINBOW

Oft when the heavens are darkest with the storm
A wondrous rainbow in the sky appears.
Oft when the heart is heaviest with fears,
Hope riseth up with bright irradiant form.

FOUR—LEAFED CLOVER

Four-leafed clover, I do not ask of thee
To bring me gold, or bright gems from the sea,
But rather bring me wealth of heart and mind;
These are the treasures that I fain would find.

SWEET MAY! COME BACK AGAIN

Sweet May! Sweet May! come back again;
   'Tis long since thou hast smiled.
Bring back thy gentle showers of rain,
   Thy fragrant flowerets wild.

Bring back the laughter of thy rills,
   The hum of drowsy bees,
The verdant freshness of the hills,
   The bud bespangled trees.

Bring back thy songsters' liquid flood
   Of music soft and low,
Bring back the sweet arbutus bud
   That blossoms down below.

Bring back each harbinger of spring.
   Of happy summer day.
Let every voice of nature sing —
   " I would 'twas always May."

Sweet May! Sweet May! come back again;
   'Tis long since thou hast smiled.
Bring back thy sweet and silent reign
   Of beauties soft and mild.

Bring back thy converse's gentle flow;
   Those happy laughing eyes;

Upon thy cheeks that tinted glow,
The blush of evening skies.

Bring back the sunshine of my heart,—
That smile upon my face.
Bring back each gentle winning art,
That made thee queen of grace.

Bring back each harbinger of bliss,
And scatter all my fear.
Of all the seasons, love I this,
When thou, sweet May, art here.

MORNING ON THE RIVER

'Tis morning on the river broad and deep,
The fair Connecticut so dear to me,
That through the Hadley meadows slow doth
creep,
Upon its journey to the distant sea,
A silver mist like to a fleecy cloud
Is floating where the fair-faced lilies hide,
And to its verdant bank the mountains crowd
To view their grandeur in the sleeping tide.

Now morning sunlight breaks upon the mist,
Faint seen at first but ever growing clear,
Like to the hidden smile behind a tear,
Until the tender beams have gently kissed
Away each trace of tears from Nature's eyes
And left her free to smile through cloudless
skies.

35

SPRINGTIME IN OLD HADLEY

Soft is the air when first the robin sings
Among the budding elms, and far he flings
The bold triumphant strain of other days
Across the field.   How changed are all earth's
    ways!
What floral beauty springs and bursts, and swells
In all her fields and lanes, and distant dells,
How birds, and brooks and bees, the whole day
        long
Flood all the walks of earth with happy song!
What subtle sweetness fills the fields and woods
When Nature recreates her solitudes;
And in the street, upon the giant trees,
The young leaves rustle in their ecstacies;
Awhile the elms, by springtime scantly drest,
Stand grandly forth, half hidden, yet confessed.

COMMUNION WITH NATURE

I hold this true — it is not solitude
Alone to wander through the trackless wood,
To pierce the deepest dells of spruce and pines,.
Where overhead the fair clematis twines,
Where 'neath your feet the soft moss sinks and
    swells,
More fair than Persian rugs or rich Brussels!
To climb the rugged steeps where stately stand
Like giant sentries to the lower land

The lordly oaks, more spreading than the pine,
Upon whose trunks the wild grape clusters shine;
What sky-born palace of the ancient time,
Relumed by limnel brush, or poet's rhyme,
Can match this peerless palace of the trees?
With roof and dome and tower and graceful frieze
All fashioned with a patience and an art,
Through centuries, that wrought each tiny part.

Let rich men boast their beds of softest down,
Upon the woodland moss I lay me down,
Where flowers and ferns and grass all interlace,
To make my weary head a resting place.
There far above me for a frescoed wall,
The woodland green is stretching over all,
Save where the friendly branches parting high,
Have left a place to view the summer sky.
From bough to bough the nimble squirrel springs,
And in each tree a plumed minstrel sings;
Among the fallen leaves are busy ants,
Rich treasures to the mind that knows their
    haunts,
And loves to watch them build their little domes,
And blend in one a thousand happy homes;
Or see the spider spin his rainbow gauze,
Obedient to some hidden unknown laws.

But if I lacked companions in the wood,
The forest stream would woo me to its flood,

For like this torrent fleeing from its home,
Impatient of delay I love to roam;
Down stony steeps to plunge in mad career,
Or walk beside it, running deep and clear,
To saunter with it through the woodland glen,
And dream apace afar from haunts of men,
But ever onward to the boundless sea,
To enter there and know its mystery.

SWEET CLARIBEL

Sweet Claribel, we called her Nature's child,
  Because she was a child of many moods;
  She loved the flowers, the meadows, and the
      woods,
But most of all the birds that caroled wild.

Her azure eyes, were ever deep and mild
  Like summer skies; her lips were cherry buds;
  She laughed more sweetly than the brook that
      floods
The mill, and all was sunshine when she smiled.

To-day she sleeps, and o'er her lowly grave
The cactus blooms, and fair palmettos wave, —
  But does she know the skies are wondrous blue?
It cannot be she heard what robin said,
Or sees the flowers that cluster round her head;
  She'd wake, and come up laughing if she knew.

TWO MOURNERS

My golden robin built his nest
  Upon a shady linden tree,
  Then sought afar o'er wood and lea
And found the bird he loved the best.

I built a cottage for my guest,
  A little maid who cared for me,
  And there we lived so happily,
Her golden head upon my breast.

The wind grew wroth one summer night
  And tost the nestlings from the tree,
  And wrecked my cottage by the sea,
And crushed the flower of my delight; —
  Another nest fronts wind and rain,
  But I shall never build again.

TWO WINDS

The north wind breathes his bitter stinging
  breath,
And all the little flowers fall down in death;
The south wind whispers over field and plain,
And every tender bud comes back again.

Golden sunlight on a rye-field softly
Gleaming when the summer day is waning;
Bathing all the field in heavenly glory,
Flooding it with mellow amber light.
Far away the verdure of the hilltops
Rises up to meet the summer sky,
And the great white ships that sail the heavens
Drift against them but they do not perish
Like the ships that sail the treacherous sea.
Among the nodding heads the busy bee
Is searching for the sweetness of the flowers,
Just as mortals look for joy and gladness
Among the brambles in the field of life.
Here a swath of golden grain is lying
Telling of the farmer's life of toiling,
And the children in the distant farmhouse
That he labors here so hard to feed.
There the grain in graceful stacks is standing,
Telling of the store that must be gathered
E'er the winter comes with sleet and snow.
And these are nature's wondrous fields and skies,
Her trees, her flowers, her grain fields, and her
    fruit,
And her richness and her wondrous beauty,
All are man's and to him freely given,
He the rightful lord of all creation
And the highest, noblest work of heaven.

So he who paints one page from Nature's book
With Nature's art, has painted God and Heaven.

PEBBLES AND SHELLS

A BREATH

Out of the garden came a little breeze,
Rich with the scent of budding flowers and trees;
So sweet the breath, that by me idly went,
My aching heart was filled with sweet content.

THE SEASONS

Spring is a laughing girl with azure eyes,
Summer the dreamy maiden grown more wise,
Autumn is womanhood, with joy, and pain,
And Winter age, when life begins to wane.

THE ICE-FLOE

The ice-floe drifting from the northern pole,
But shows a little o'er the rolling seas;
So he who thinks he knows life's mysteries,
But sees a portion of the mighty whole.

THE AURORA

Only a flush upon the northern sky,
Then suddenly the heavens open wide,
And flames with green and gold, and crimson
    dyed,
Leap fiercely forth, then slowly sink, and die.

Poor is the prince, though Croesus' countless
   gold,
And all the priceless gems of earth's dark mold,
   Be lavished at his feet, if he ne'er sees
   The beauty of this world of mysteries.
Rich is the swain beside this man of gold,
Though poor his purse, his garments torn and old,
   Whose eyes can see, and heart can understand
   The wondrous joys of Nature's lavish hand.

For 'tis not wealth, or fame, or power, or birth,
That gives man's soul its heritage of worth,
   It is the mind to grasp, the heart to feel
   The whole of life, its beauty, and its weal,
To draw pure pleasure sweet for age or youth
From out the founts of God's eternal truth.

To live like yonder robin in her nest
And know that all that happeneth is best,
   To learn a lesson from yon hive of bees,
   That draw their sweetness from the flowers
      and trees,
To read fair Nature's book on mount and dell,
And lend thy soul unto her silent spell,
   To feel the law, the truth, the happy plan
   That bindeth Nature to the heart of man.

THE MOUNTAIN TO THE PINE

Thou tall, majestic monarch of the wood,
  That standeth where no wild vines dare to
  creep,
Men call thee old, and say that thou hast stood
  A century upon my rugged steep;
Yet unto me thy life is but a day,
  When I recall the things that I have seen,—
The forest monarchs that have passed away
  Upon the spot where first I saw thy green;
For I am older than the age of man,
  Or all the living things that crawl or creep,
  Or birds of air, or creatures of the deep;
I was the first dim outline of God's plan,—
  Only the waters of the restless sea
  And the infinite stars in heaven are old to
  me.

JUNE AND OCTOBER

June and October come to us and reign,
  Abide with us through all the changing year
  And make this earth more fair, this life more
  dear,
Let summer sunlight flood each darksome plain,
Let autumn glory deck each lonely lane,
  And all the world be filled with songs of cheer,
  Till life shall be too full for doubt and fear.

Dark is the heart, and steeped in ceaseless pain
That cannot smile when June comes back again;
   Sad is the soul, and lonely are the ways
   That can resist October's dreamy days.
I love them both, these gentle sisters twain,—
   Sweet, smiling June. without a thought of care,
   And fair October with her chestnut hair.

NOONDAY IN SUMMER

The brazen sun is in the zenith sky,
Its summer heat has scorched earth's shady ways,
Her verdure withers 'neath its burning rays,
And fragile flow'rets fade, and droop, and die.
The cooling winds are e'en too faint to sigh,
And all the leaves upon the trees are still,
The busy bee goes droning o'er the hill
To gather sweetness from the blooming rye.
The brook still sings its drowsy lullaby,
And shrill the locust wakes his noonday lay,
But still the sunflower drinks the burning ray
And turns its face up fearless to the sky,
And hollyhocks and poppies look more fair
Beneath the glamour of the noonday glare.

BY HILL AND VALE

Through hill and vale life's winding way is laid
  By stony walks and highways fresh and sweet,
  And oft the cruel stones shall cut thy feet
As one by one life's countless steps are made;
And some at noon shall rest them in the shade
  Upon the summit of achievements steep,
  And some at morn shall lay them down to
    sleep,
When life is fresh, in indolence's cool shade;
And some are strong of heart and not dismayed
  By all the dangers of life's varied way, —
  With swift impetuous feet that naught can stay
They journey on; and some are sore afraid, —
  But still they hurry on, by hills and vales
  Until the sun goes down and day-light fails.

THE MOUNTAIN AND THE STREAM

  " Oh, restless stream, why do you hurry?
    This peaceful world is not for worry;
    Pray, stop with me and view the scene —
    The tranquil hills, and meadows green."

  " I cannot stop, I flow forever,
    For I must be a mighty river;
    You ne'er can feel and ne'er can know
    The boundless joy it is to flow.
    So while you stand, majestic, grand,
    I hurry along, with ceaseless song
    To ocean's strand."

PEBBLES AND SHELLS

EROSION

Even the little waves that idly dance
   Against the cliff, will crumble it to sand;
   And so, with ceaseless toil, the slightest hand
May wear away the walls of circumstance.

THE AFTERGLOW

After the day is done, the passing light
Sheddeth a halo round the feet of night;
So, after death, a noble life may shed
Soft radiance where they that live must tread.

NATURE'S PALACE

What courts of stone can match the deep green
     wood
   Where verdant oaks and maples spreading
     meet,
   With ferns, and flowers, and mosses for the
     feet,
And for man's din, sweet Nature's solitude.

THE LANGUAGE OF THE LEAVES

When in the deep green woods I idly walk,
And all the little leaves begin to talk
Among the branches of the forest trees,—
I think how filled is earth with mysteries.

AT NATURE'S FEET

I love to be a child at Nature's feet,
   And on her mossy footstool sit and dream,
   Awhile the wild wind and the mountain stream
Delight mine ears with music wondrous sweet.
I love to note the marvelous conceit
   With which she hides her beauty and her grace,
   And decks with care each lone forsaken place,
And fills the sea with beauties so replete.
O, Nature! fill me with thy sweet delight,
   And let me learn thy matchless minstrelsy,
   The music of the stars, the sky, the sea,
The peaks, the plains,— that I may sing aright;
   Then will I wake the nations with a song
   That men shall hear and feel and ponder long.

NIAGARA

Niagara, sublime, eternal, grand,
Rolling thy thunderous torrent ceaselessly;
Thou art one drop from out the boundless sea,
That resteth in the hollow of God's hand.

LITTLE THINGS

There is no blade of grass but has some power,
And silently it groweth, hour by hour;
There is no life, however mean or small
But addeth something to God's mighty whole.

TO AN ARTIST AT HER EASEL

It was a fair October day,
  The distant hills were gold and brown,
  And yet the heavens could not frown,
Though Summer's joys had passed away.
Upon the grass I musing lay,
  And watched an artist's magic skill
  That slowly formed a distant hill;
And, in my heart I longed to say,
If thou couldst paint the eager face,
  The parted lips, the fevered brow,
  The earnest gaze that fronts me now,
Thy face would surely grow apace,
  I swear it by my truthful pen
  Thy name would be immortal then.

THE HARVEST

Behold the golden fields of ripening grain,
The fair fruition of the sun and rain,
  And man's poor heritage of tears and cares.
  And in the golden grain behold the tares;
Poor human tares,—'tis part of my belief,—
God will forget and bind you in His sheaf.

SONG OF THE ROBIN

Upon the lofty maple tree
  I hear a robin singing —
His rich and happy melody
  Through all the woods is ringing,—
Cheer up! cheer up! all things clear up,
We are merry, cherry! cheery!

The sun has slowly sunk to rest,
  The shades of night are falling;
And from his bough beside the nest
  The robin still is calling,—
Cheer up! cheer up! all things clear up,
We are merry, cherry! cheery!

Now one by one the stars appear,
  The evening winds are sighing
And robin's song of hope and cheer
  Is slowly, gently dying,—
Cheer up! cheer up! all things clear up,
We are merry, cherry! cheery!

The deepest shades of night have come
  And robin's song is ended,
But in my heart with doubt and gloom,
  His hope and cheer have blended.
Cheer up! cheer up! all things clear up,
We are merry, cherry! cheery!

OCTOBER

October reigns o'er all the dreamy hills —
Awake my soul, and lift thy voice in praise,
And sing the glory of autumnal days,
And voice the gladness of the heart that thrills,
When to the brim the cup of nature fills.

Each mountain range is wrapped in dreamy haze
And through the gentle veil the sun's bright rays
Are half subdued, and yet the power that chills
On vine and bush has set its seal in blood
And far and near the pennons of the wood
Stream like a conflagration to the sky;
Each blade and leaf, each tiny emerald thing
Unto the pyre has brought its offering
And laid it there amid the flames to die.

THE LAST FAIR DAY

It was the last fair day of all the year,
Halfway between the realms of heat and cold,
When days are short and Boreas is bold
And summer fields and woods are bare and sere;
But all that there was left of warmth and cheer
This day had caught within its fleecy fold
Of summer sky, and o'er the frozen wold
The lancers of the cold fled back in fear

Oh! how the glad sun warmed the frozen earth,
Making her pulseless heart to beat again,
Dancing his sunbeams over hill and plain
Until it seemed like Summer's second birth,
But e'er his orb had even time to dim
The night and cold fell like a pall on him.

AUTUMNAL HOPES

In dark December look to spring,
And learn to hear the robin sing
  Upon his unbuilt nest;
In sorrow teach thy lips to say—
I know this pain will pass away,
  And I will see 'twas best.

PEBBLES AND SHELLS

TIME

Time is a bird that wings with ceaseless flight
Over the land, nor rests by day or night;
You mark its form against the sky of dawn
Then dream apace, and night comes softly on.

THE CLOVER BLOSSOM

Slender and pale, and hidden in the grass,
So that you scarce can see it as you pass,
The clover stands,—but every wild bee knows
'Tis sweeter far than any blushing rose.

ROILED

The placid brooklet ran with limped flood —
The angry stream grew dark with sticks and
    mud —
So anger darkens e'en the brightest face
And takes from fair humanity its grace.

A LOVER

The honey-bee, through sunny hours
Goes courting all the sweetest flowers,—
Into their hearts he slyly slips
And steals sweet nectar from their lips.

Faintly the feeble sun streamed through the gray
That hung the heavens, and marked the waning
      day,
  Then sank from sight; we could not see him go,
  Only a sickly streak of yellow glow
Revealed his path.   Then fell the shades of
      night,—
But not as they are wont, with silver light
  From peaceful stars, or radiance from the moon
  That make the winter night more fair than
      noon;
But with dark clouds that wrapped the fields in
      gloom,
Until the night was dark as Sodom's doom.

Then woke the wild wind in the leafless trees
And called the Frost King from his frozen seas,
  And hand in hand, they scoured the frozen
      earth,
  And peeped in at the panes, where joy and
      mirth
Had gathered round some cosy kitchen hearth;
And at the sight the wild wind roared in wrath,
  Awhile the bitter Frost King tried each
      crack,—
  But soon the bright fire drove him panting
      back;

Yet still he lingered by the window frame
And on its smooth glass wrote his mystic name.

Then through the cellar wall went creeping in,
To nip the rosy apples in their bin,
Or freeze the golden pumpkins on the floor,
With spiteful heart to spoil the winter store;
But ever and anon comes back again
To peep in at the frosty window pane,
And, if the fire upon the hearth burns low,
He creeps into the room, and chills it so
That soon the revelers draw near the fire
And stir the coals and pile the fuel higher.
And all this time, the wild wind shrieks and
groans,
Or bellows down the chimney top, or moans
Among the trees, or with a sudden roar,
Comes rudely knocking at the cottage door.
Thus goes the night, until on field and town,
The feathery snow comes softly sifting down,
Spreading its mantle o'er the field and wood,
Folding the earth in winter's solitude.

Then morning breaks, and on the young day's
cheek
There comes a flush and then a crimson streak,
And soon the great sun shining clear and bright
Mounts o'er the hills and floods the world
with light.

How strange the scene,—the winds no longer
    blow
And quiet reigns; but how the wind-tossed snow
    Disguises mother earth, until things seem
    To be transfigured by some mystic dream.
The firs are spotless white and bending low
Beneath their heavy load of new made snow;
    The regal elm-trees lift their mighty arms,
    With snow and frost upon their leafless palms
And stand like giants in the morning light,
Their shaggy bark half showing through the
    white;
    Each fence and hedge has caught the feathery
    down—
The garden gate-post wears a regal crown;
The rose-bush too, is loaded by the storm,
And every shrub has changed its old time form.

But soon the heavy teams, with boys and men,
    Will come to break the drifted roads again
And pierce the deepest drifts and pile them high
And let the merry sleighing party by;
    For well New England young folks love the
    air,
    The frost, the wind, the cold, the snow's white
    glare
And all the bitter cold and nipping frost,
But lends enchantment to the merry coast.

The great sun wheels his course and night
    draws near
For winter days are short though sharp and
    clear.
Again the restless wind begins to moan
Among the trees in cheerless monotone
    And shake the new snow from the loaded
        boughs
    And fill the tracks just broken by the plows.
Swiftly the shadows lengthen o'er the snow
And one one by one the constellations show;
    Then night comes down and earth fantastic
        lies
    Beneath its cold star-gleaming winter skies.

THE WHIP-POOR-WILL

The soft, deep gloom of night on vale and hill
Half hid the glories of the summer skies,
And pearly tears, the dewdrops of the eyes,
Obscured the dusky forms that lingered still.
And while I watched, a cry pathetic, shrill,
As 'twere the voice of some forgotten wrong,
With three sad notes the burden of the song
Filled all the night with strains of " Whip-poor-
    will! "
A simple song beside the lark's mad flight,
A worthless song of wild, rude minstrelsy,

But those three notes revealed anew to me
Life's mystery, its breadth, its depth, its height—
And yet, I trow he heard the lark that day
And knew he sang a rude, uncultured lay.

THE FROZEN STREAM

The cold wind swept the fields and forest o'er
And all the little leaves came fluttering down,
The reeds and grasses turned to sombre brown
And robin's happy song was heard no more.

The little streamlet heard the wild wind's roar
And saw the azure sky grow dark with dread;
Then built a palace for his houseless head,
And sealed it tight and locked the crystal door.
Gay colored pebbles formed the palace floor,
And every mystic form of fairy lore
Was fashioned in that clear transparent dome.

In stormy days it felt no winds that blew,
In sunny hours the light of heaven came through
To cheer the little streamlet in its home.

THE FLICKER

Gay crested tenant of the deep wild woods,
Oft have I heard thee wake these solitudes
  Where quiet loves to dwell, with lightning
    stroke,

(Holding with clinging claws to elm or oak,)
Until the echoes of thy sturdy whacks
Gave back a sound like to the woodsman's axe;
While thou didst drive thy beak, with point like
steel,
Deep in the wood to find thy morning meal.

PICTURES ON THE PANE

The frost gnomes came one Winter's night
While slumber held its grateful reign,
And wrote upon my window pane;
Then stole away with morning light.
I sought to read the scroll aright
Yet had no art to understand
The meaning of so strange a hand;
But when the morning sun grew bright,
The picture melted into rain
And then its mystery was plain.
It was a symbol of man's years,
That set in colors seeming fair,
Beneath life's noonday heat and glare
Oft proves but vanity and tears.

WHY ?

Along life's walk the shadows fall
Because the world is full of light,
And if the world was not so bright
The shadows would not come at all.

THE SUNSET

Slowly the mighty sun with 'fulgent ray
Goes sliding down into the crimson west,
Leaving the embers of the dying day
    Still burning where the ragged cloud-rifts rest ;
Pauseth a moment on the mountain's line,
    Staining its verdure like a warrior's breast,
Then sinks from sight, and mellow after-shine
    Fringes with gold the crimson snow clouds'
      crest.
Now fades the gorgeous glory of the sky
    And deep cool shadows steal o'er vale and hill,
Even the trembling aspen's leaf is still
    And nothing stirs the quiet of the night
Save when the marsh-frog pipes his shrilly cry,
    Or some lone night-bird wings his whirring
      flight.

PEBBLES AND SHELLS

THE STARS

The stars are as bright in the heavens to-night
As though they had just been born,
Instead of as old as the shimmering light
That broke on creation's morn.

THE BOBOLINK

Deep fountain of unstinted song
That springs and gurgles all day long,
Thy lilting song is purest art
For all thy strains are of the heart.

FLORA'S CALL

Come up, come up, my little buds,
The snow is gone and spring is here.
The robin sings his song of cheer
And you must grace the fields and woods.

ARBUTUS

Fair fragrant buds that nestle in the grass
And hide from me so closely as I pass,
Thou art an emblem of true charity,
That bends its head and hides that none may see.

THE NORTH STAR

Jewel in heaven, where all rare jewels are,.
Night after night thy steady glow we see,
Would that my soul might find for it a star,
So fair, so bright, so full of constancy.

A WINTER'S NIGHT

It is a cold star-gleaming Winter's night —
All things are ice-bound like the frozen mill—
The great white moon comes stalking o'er the hill'
And floods the scene with cold unearthly light;
The leafless trees are hung with jewels bright
And every twig is set with magic skill
And fringed with frost that speaks the winter's.
　　　chill;
The darkling pines are robed in spotless white,
Their loaded branches nod like warriors' plumes.
And cast their shadows in the forest's glooms;.
Far in the wood with melancholy moan
The wind awakes its cheerless monotone
Then dies away and all is cold and still.

AFTER THE STORM

Down from the frozen clouds fell sleet and rain,.
Over the wintry fields and forest hoar
The wild winds swept with melancholy roar,.
Awhile the frost bedecked the window pane;

At morn the sun resumed his tranquil reign,
  The fair earth smiled through all her frozen
    tears
  And Winter's face revealed his secret fears.
How gorgeous was the scene,—each field and
    lane
  Was paved with purest pearls and sparkling
    gems,
  The darkling furs were hung with diadems,
And every leafless vine was fringed with frost;
  While Phoebus' rays on ice gems strangely
    made
Revealed their rainbow hues; all without cost
  The walks of earth like heaven's streets were
    laid.

A HAVEN

My life was launched upon a stormy sea,
Without a pilot for its shallow bark,
To front the storm, the lightnings, and the dark,
The winds and tides that breed adversity
And batter with the waves unceasingly.
And I have fought the elements until
The restless sea has worn away my will,
E'en as it wears the rocks, and conquered me;
And now whene'er a lighthouse lifts its form
Above the outline of the dreamy coast
While my poor bark is rudely tempest tossed,

I long to shield me from the cruel storm
In some fair haven by the peaceful shore
To cast an anchor till life's storms are o'er.

"THE CIRCLE OF THE GOLDEN YEAR"

JANUARY

The earth is white, the air is sharp and clear,
When joyous bells ring in the glad New Year;
   With all its joy and grief, the old year's out—
   We look not back, but welcome with a shout
The glad New Year, for all its days are ours
To live, to strive, and prove our manhoods'
    powers.

FEBRUARY

But when the days begin to show their length,
Then winter hoar puts forth his utmost strength;
   Then deeper, and still deeper, falls the snow,
   And fiercer, and still fiercer wild winds blow,
Until the fields and woods are piled with drifts
And scarce a day the leaden storm cloud lifts.

MARCH

In March the Winter's last wild throes are seen,
With days of sunlight coming in between—
   A strange commingling blast of heat and cold
   And howling winds that sweep the barren wold,
The bleakest month of all the varied year,
But, at its close, the bare brown hills appear.

Then April comes with sunshine and with
    showers
To start the buds and wake the sleeping flowers.
  Along the fields there comes a touch of green—
  Upon the trees the bursting buds are seen,
And bluebirds bright, with robins blithely sing
And all things feel the thrilling touch of spring.

MAY

In May we tread again the pleasant woods
And search the fields for sweet arbutus buds;
  'Tis then the shad puts on its spotless sheen
  And daffodils and adder-tongues are seen —
The orchards, too, are radiant with bloom
And all the air is filled with sweet perfume.

JUNE

Oh! June, thou month of joy and love and
    peace
Of boundless skies soft flecked with clouds of
    fleece,
  Of balmy winds that whisper of content—
  With hedge and lawn and garden radiant
With all the sweetest, fairest flowers that blow—
Oh! June, dear June! how can I let thee go?

JULY

When July comes the broad and fertile plain
Afar and near is rich with waving grain,
   With wheat and oats and fields of nodding
      rye
   And growing corn with streamers waving
      high—
While from the hayfield comes the noisy song
Of cutter-bar and tedder all day long.

AUGUST

When August comes with cloudless brazen sky
Then oft the fragile flowerets droop and die,
   And e'en the fresh maize curls its verdant
      leaves
   Yet gives a promise of the golden sheaves —
And all the birds like revellers grow merry
On garden fruit and many a luscious berry.

SEPTEMBER

The summer grain has all been harvested
And stowed away in mow and loft and shed
   The corn is in the shock and golden fruit
   Is ripe upon the trees, and vine and root
Have yielded up their yearly offering,
And well redeemed the promises of spring.

OCTOBER

Soft hazy skies o'erarch the dreamy world
When Autumn's gorgeous pennon is unfurled,
   It almost seems that June is here again
   So deep the joy that fills the heart and brain—
And then there comes the falling of a leaf,
Though slight the sound it stirs the heart with
      grief.

NOVEMBER

Sad melancholy month, with tearful skies,
When all the glad earth's verdure smitten lies —
   When all the happy birds have southward
      flown
   And through the leafless trees the shrill winds
      moan,
Whistling a requiem for Nature's dead,
Filling the mournful skies with clouds like lead.

DECEMBER

Earth's sombre garb is soft with new made snow
When Christmas brings the thoughts of long ago;
   Upon the cheerful hearth the Yule-log glows
   And though the skies be dark with falling
      snows
It throws no shade upon the Christmas glee,
For Christ is King and reigns from sea to sea.

POEMS OF WAR AND
PATRIOTISM

HOW "FIGHTING JOE HOOKER" TOOK LOOKOUT MOUNTAIN

Know you the tale of a battle won
  Some thirty years ago,
On a mountain top, when the Autumn sun
  In the west was sinking low ?

It was a fight that the watching throng
  Were destined not to see,
For the men went up five thousand strong
  Under the canopy

Of God's free sky, through the fleecy clouds
  That overhung the plain,
And the eager eyes of the watchful crowds
  Strained after them in vain.

'Twas like a storm on a darksome night —
  This battle in the clouds,
With the thunder's roll and the leven's light
  Among the mountain's shrouds.

The sky was dark on that Autumn day
  The air was damp and cold,
But the fields and woods in their mantle lay
  Of crimson and of gold;

Fresh laurel grew on the mountain's side
  Among the evergreen
And the granite rocks with the verdure vied
  To beautify the scene.

They come—they come o'er the verdant plain
    With flags but not with drum,
By the broad highway and the narrow lane,
    They come, they come, they come!

They round the base of the mountain tall,
    Unnoticed by the foe,
On the southern side of its rugged wall
    They stand to strike the blow.

" Advance! my boys," is the clear command
    It comes from " Fighting Joe,"
And the men go up to the Rebels' stand,
    As only patriots go.

They climb the rocks and the frowning cliffs
    Like Sparta's patriotic sons,
And they scale the steep through the friendly
      rifts
    Up to the Rebel guns.

Then fell a blight like the breath of Hell,
    Out of the mountain banks,
With a storm of lead and a Rebel yell
    They fell upon our ranks;

We drove them back up the mountain walls,
    And gave them shot for shot,
Till the air was filled with our shrieking balls
    And e'en the winds were hot.

The battle raged for a bloody hour,
  And neither had the best,
Till just as the night was beginning to lower,
  When Hooker gained the crest.

He swept the foe from the mountain's crown,
  And on its utmost crag,
Just as the radiant sun went down,
  Planted the starry flag.

A moment more and our signal gun
  Woke echoes in the glen,
And the army knew that the fight was won
  By Hooker's gallant men.

A PRISONER IN CHAINS

In prison and in chains he stands,
Within a dark and narrow cell,
And many sentries guard him well,
But they have only bound his hands —
His spirit moves a thousand clans,
His glory gleams on shining shields,
A mighty kingdom quakes and reels,
And freedom shouts in tyrant lands.

Such is the power of noble deeds,
That where one soul for freedom dies
A thousand steel-clad warriors rise,
To follow where the martyr leads.

The clanging of one prison chain
Oft breaks a mighty despot's reign.

THE LIVING DEAD

When Freedom calls for heroes in her cause
And all the air is ringing with applause,
To charge the foe, e'en to the cannon's breath,
And there lay down thy life is noblest death.

When thou art dead to all that life can give,
To take thy place within the ranks and live
And move as others do, is nobler far,
And on the soul it leaves a deeper scar —

There thou wert dead and all thy glory shone,
Here thou art dead, and e'en thy death unknown.

HOW MASSA LINKUM CAME

You chillun ebber hear me tell
  About ole Richmond town ;
How 'fore de closement ob de war
  De Linkum troops came down ?

I tell you, chilluns, dem was days
  Ole Moses don't forget,
Though thirty years hab trabbled by
  I feel that 'sperence yet.

Dat time de Linkum sojers come
    A marchin' up the street,
Wid all dar regermentums on
    An' music mighty sweet.

Den how de darkies shouted loud
    " De Juberlee hab come!"
An' how de chilluns peel dar eyes
    To see de big base drum.

Den how de sojers marched along,
    Dar muskets gleamin' bright,
An' how de music made us feel
    Right pow'ful for de fight.

But what I gwine to tell dis crowd's
    How Massa Linkum came,
De man dat made your mammies free
    By signin' ob his name.

How 'fore he brought de army down
    He dun come down to see
How Richmond looked and try to find
    What come ob Massa Lee.

One day we heard it whispered round
    Mars Linkum's comin' here;
An' Massa Davis heard it too,
    An' dat's what make him clear.

De news had come mysterious —
　　We didn't think 'twas true,
But I was jes a watchin' out
　　With nothin' much to do.

It was de blessed Sabbath morn,
　　De ribber sparklin bright,
An' all de country fresh an' green
　　An' smilin' in de light.

An' I was sittin' on de warves
　　Jes where de sun came down,
A gazin' at the distant hills
　　Beyond the sleepy town,

When down de ribber far away
　　I see a little smoke,
An' on de air so strangely still
　　A tug boat screechin' broke.

Dat didn't 'sturb me.—not at all
　　Dat squeelin' ribber brat;
Dat not de way Mars Linkum come,
　　He make more noise den dat.

But bye and bye dat tug boat came
　　An' bunted at the wharf
An' den I saw fo' genelums
　　Make ready to get off.

Dey came a walkin' up de plank
  A kinder lookin' roun'
Like dey was strangers in de place
  An' didn't know de town.

Dey was a right smart lookin' crowd,
  I didn't mind 'em all,
But one had gold upon his coat,
  An' one was mighty tall.

But pretty soon dey comes along
  Right near to where I sat,
An' one ob dem steps up to me
  A liftin' ob his hat;

"Hallo, Uncle Tom," the gemmun said,
  "How would you like to see
The President ob dis great land
  The man who made you free?"

"See Massa Linkum! sah," I said,
  "My eyes a growin' dim,
Ob all de men de Lord has made
  I'd rudder look at him."

"Well,— dar he is,"— de gemmun said,
  I saw de man he meant —
De tallest one upon de right,
  He was de President.

I 'low dat statement took me back,
  A moment I was dumb,
An' then I shouted, '' Hallelujah!
  Massa Linkum's come!''

You better bet dey heard dat yell —
  I fotched it long and loud,
An' in a moment more de street
  Was swarmin' wid de crowd;

An' ebery chile took up de cry
  An' shouted — '' Kingdom come!
Hallelujah! hallelujah!
  Massa Linkum's come!''

An' ebery moment dat went by
  De shoutin' grew more loud.
An' roun' dem four de darkies swarmed
  As thick as dey could crowd.

An' in de midst ob all dat throng,
  A smilin' his consent,
A lookin' mighty grand and tall,
  Still stood de President.

'Twas just about dat time, I guess,
  'Long come old Parson Jake;
He made his way right through de crowd
  A swingin' ob a rake.

Right up to Massa Linkum's side
  Dat no-count Parson came,
A bowin' like a turkey-cock
  An' callin' him by name.

He shook de President by de hand,
  An' den I heard him say:
'' We're mighty glad dat you hab come,
  Mars Linkum,— let us pray.''

I tell you chillun, I was scared
  For our ole Parson den,
To hear him talkin' dat a way
  To such official men.

I spec' Mars Linkum dun get mad
  An' knock dat nigger flat,
Or mebbe kick him in de shins,
  Or smash his Sunday hat.

But Massa Linkum only smiled
  At what dat Parson said,
An' took his big tall beaver off
  An' den bowed down his head.

Den Parson Jake, he knelt right down
  Upon dat dirty street,
An' prayed a pra'r dat fairly took
  Dis nigger off his feet.

He t'anked de Lord dat he had seen
   Our sorrow and distress,
An' brought us up, all safe an' sound,
   Out ob de Wilderness.

Dat he had sent Mars Linkum round
   To lead us in de dark,
To part de Jordan's rushing wave
   An' smite de solid rock.

He prayed de Lord to bless dis land,
   De white folks an' de black,
An' send de dove of peace around
   An' bring ole Massa back.

He axed de Lord to bless de men
   Who fought to free de slaves,
He prayed de Lord to comfort dem
   Down where de cotton waves.

I b'lieve he prayed for ebryting
   In dis here blessed land.
Wid Massa Linkum standin' by,
   A bowin' thar so grand.

De pickaninnies stood so still
   You t'ink dey made o' stone,
Dey didn't speak, nor move, nor breeve
   Until dat pra'r was done;

An' den dey broke into a shout
  Dat mought hab woke John Brown,
An' cheered until I t'ink de noise
  Would bring de heabens down.

An' Massa Linkum waved his hand
  In answer to dem cheers;
His countenance was shinin' bright
  His cheeks were wet wid tears.

" De Lord forgive an' bless us all,—
  De libin' an' de dead,
An' bring sweet peace unto de land — "
  Mars Linkum husky said.

" An' make de norf an' souf as one
  An' wipe away dar tears
An' fill de nation wid his love
  Thro' all de comin' years."

An' while he spoke he stretched his han's
  Above dat 'cited crowd;
I knowed de Lord would hear dat pra'r, —
  I tell you we was proud.

An' den de fo' went up de street
  To music ob de band,
An' all de darkies marchin' wid
  De President ob de land.

An' dat's de story ob de way
  Dat Massa Linkum come,
Widout de marchin' ob de troops,
  Or beatin' ob de drum.

An' tho' black Mose is growin' ole,
  An' foolish some folks say;
He don't forget de t'ings he saw
  Dat wondrous Sabbath day.

LA GILLOTINE

I see a square where that dread engine stands,
And gathered round a cruel vengeful throng,
Made blind by centuries of want and wrong
To truth and right, with blood upon their hands.
Amid the throng one noble figure stands,
With regal form and features clear and strong,
Indifferent to curses deep and long
Heaped on her head by Paris' motly bands.
A moment e'er she dies she lifts her head
To view the form of liberty that cries
Eternally to God against man's lies;
The whole world knows the glowing words she
    said.
O liberty! unto thy holy name
What crimes are linked to hide their burning
    shame.

REVEILLE SONG

The soldier slept in his guarded tent,
    The night was nearly done,
The twinkling stars in the firmament
    Were fading one by one;
He dreamed of home and his waiting wife
    And heaved a long drawn breath,
Of the battlefield and its sick'ning strife
    And agonies of death. —

Awake! awake! 'tis the warning drum,
Fall into line, for the foemen come.
Awake! awake! 'tis the warning drum;
Fall into line, for the foemen come.

The soldier wakes with a sudden start
    And reaches for his gun,
'Midst crashing shell and shrieking shot
    He fights till day is done.
At set of sun, on the slippery banks,
    Pierced by a score of balls,
The foremost man in the foremost ranks,
    The brave young soldier falls.

Charge on! charge on! is the stirring cry,
The day is won, for the foemen fly.
Charge on! charge on! is the stirring cry;
The day is won, for the foemen fly.

The soldier sleeps in " his low green tent,"
   Encoffined in the mold,
The selfsame stars in the firmament
   Are shining as of old.
The same dear flag that he loved so well
   Above him still doth wave,
And the sweet wild rose and the asphodel
   Are growing on his grave.

Asleep, asleep, is the soldier there,
And he'll not wake for a martial air.
Asleep, asleep, is the soldier there
And he'll not wake for a martial air.

The soldier wakes with a sudden thrill,
   The reveille of God
Has sounded forth from the throned hills
   And burst the matted sod.
An Angel read from the records then
   On leaves of flaming gold,
They gave their lives for their fellow men,
   As Jesus did of old.

Abide with me, is the Lord's reply,
And dwell for aye with the saints on high.
Abide with me, is the Lord's reply,
And dwell for aye with the saints on high.

THAT LAST WILD CHARGE AT GETTYSBURG!

That last wild charge to scale the height —
It was a grand, yet awful sight!
  Though thirty years have passed away,
  It seems to me but yesterday —
That hour we stood on gory banks
And watched Lee's gray-clad gleaming ranks
  Charge out across the peaceful plain,
  From whence they turned not back again.

Fair Gettysburg lies far below,
Beside the creeks still peaceful flow,
  Upon the meadows o'er the way
  The harvesters are making hay,
And low of cattle from the hills
And liquid laughter from the rills
  And song of bird from near and far
Sound not like harbingers of war.

Out of the South, with roll of drum,
The blue and gray-clad armies come,
  Creeping along in silent files,
  Marching abreast for sixty miles,
Watching each other day and night —
Watching and waiting for the fight.
  Thus came they when the sun went down,
  And camped about the little town.

Three weary days, from height to height,
The battle rolled from morn till night;
    Three dreary days the cannon's breath
    Belched forth its messengers of death,
Till earth and sky grew dark with dread
And many thousand men lay dead —
    Then silently the remnant gray
    Closed up its ranks and stole away.

'Twas on the third day " Charge!" was said —
The day that last wild charge was led;
    They fired no shot from ten till one,
    Each gunner rested on his gun;
A breathless hush and a deathlike calm
Foretold the coming of the storm.

Then like some mighty tidal crest
That rises high above the rest
    And madly dashes on the shore
    With thund'rous shock and deaf'ning roar,
There rose a mighty sea of men
Where peaceful fields of grain had been,
    And half the Southern army wheeled
    And charged across the quiet field.

They shook the ridges with their yells —
We could not hear their bursting shells —
    They ploughed our breastworks with their
        shot —

The July air grew thick and hot—
They strewed the hillside with our dead;
They shook the vale with thund'rous tread;
   And yet no answer from the hill,
   Our grinning guns were deathly still.

But when the Rebel line swept down
Upon the road that led to town,
   The Union rank its silence broke
   And every frowning cannon spoke.

I've seen the forked lightning's play
Until the night was bright as day;
   I've heard the dreaded thunder's wrath
   That seemed to shake the very earth.
Then like the lightning's blinding flash,
Then like the thunder's deaf'ning crash,
   Three hundred cannons' vengeful ire
   Burst forth in shot and shell and fire.

A mighty flame lit earth and sky—
I saw a host of heroes die—
   I heard the crash of shattered steel—
   I felt the boulders rock and reel;
Then all the scene grew black as night,
As hotter, fiercer grew the fight.
   'Midst sick'ning smoke and flying sand,
   The dead so thick we scarce could stand,
'Midst solid shot and bursting shell

And every horror known in hell,
We fought as men ne'er fought before
And turned the tide of cruel war.

As darkness flees at break of day,
As every tempest dies away,
So ceased the storm on hill and plain,
The fall of leaden sleet and rain.
Then came a gentle evening breath
And kissed the fevered fields of death,
And blew aside the friendly screen
And showed us where the fight had been.
We saw no shattered army then,
With broken lines of flying men;
We heard no sound of rushing feet,
Of scattered corps in wild retreat;
We saw no banner rise and fall,
We heard no drum or bugle call,
Only a crimson field instead,
With an endless stretch of sleeping dead,
The Southern army widely slain,
Gone like a leaf in the hurricane.

All honor to the charge they made!
All glory to the men who stayed
That fearless charge, with a fearless stand
For Freedom and their native land!
We praise them with our mingled cheers,

We grieve them with our mingled tears,
   And a nation springs to the bugle call,
   And the starry flag floats over all.
God grant that this may ever be
The land of love and liberty,
   And that Old Glory's stripe and star
   Shall ne'er again be raised in war!

REBEL AND PATRIOT

A hero rose in armor bright
To drive a tyrant from the land;
The monarch brought his armed band
And crushed him in a single fight,
And wrong still triumphed over right.
The rebel died, his honored name
Was branded with a traitor's shame.
Another rose in greater might,
With dauntless men at his command
And drove the tyrant from the land.
The people cheered the noble deed,
And placed the crown upon his head,
The crown of him who first had bled
In freedom's cause and sown the seed.

Slow the burning sun was waning
  Where Napoleon's line had reeled,
Where the blood of France was staining
  All the verdure of the field;

Where her bravest sons were lying,
  Piled in heaps of mangled dead,
And the moaning of the dying
  Filled the air with sounds of dread;

Where the muskets' furious rattle
  Never ceased, and cannon frowned,
And the din and shock of battle
  Shook the earth for miles around;

There the Corsican had blundered,
  And his army was undone,
And the Teuton's guns had thundered,
  And the Austrian had won.

There with all her army scattered
  By the whirlwind of the fray,
And with half her legions shattered
  France had surely lost the day.

And her great commander madly
  Raving at this first defeat,
Said unto his drummer sadly,
  "Victor, beat the quick retreat."

"O my General, I have never
  Beat that shameful strain before,
At the touch my drum would wither,
  Let me sound the charge once more."

"Who would answer to the summons?"
  Then Napoleon hotly said,
"Where are all my boasted legions ?
  They are scattered, they are dead."

"If I call them they will rally,
  They are patriots, they are men,
They will come from hill and valley,
  Let me call them once again."

And these words from one so daring,
  One so young, yet truly brave,
Put to shame the heart despairing,
  And resistless courage gave.

"Sound the charge!" the general thundered,
  "Let us rally, all who can,"
And the Austrian foemen wondered
  At the daring of the man.

But the French along the valley
  Raised the cry of Bonaparte,
And they rallied to the sally
  With new courage and new heart.

Victor led them to the breastworks,
  Up the banks they saw him climb,

And the rolling of his drumsticks
To the double quick kept time.

Who could see him and not follow?
O'er the works the Frenchmen swept,.
And that last mad charge of Marlow
Long in Austria was wept;

For it turned the tide of battle,
And it filled the foe with dread,
And the rest, like frightened cattle,
O'er the hills and valleys fled.

Then they sought the little drummer
Who had led the charge so well,
In the lightnings and the glamour,
E'en into the mouth of hell.

On the works they found him lying,.
There beside his riddled drum,
Where the mangled dead and dying
Made the heart with pity numb.

He the bravest of those heroes,
With his face turned towards the foe,.
Dead to all life's joys and sorrows,
Gone where such brave spirits go.

Filled with grief and tender pity,
To the strains of Marseillaise,

Then they bore him to the city
　　Where the air was rife with praise.

There they left him and the people
　　Laid him in a soldier's grave,
Close beside St. Martin's steeple,
　　Where his country's banners wave.

And they'll not forget the story
　　Until Pity dries her tears,
And the head of Time grows hoary
　　With the burden of the years.

OUR FLAG

Red for the life blood that freely was given
　　To shield our bright banner when infamy
　　　came;
　　White for the nation that purged her dark
　　　shame,
Blue for her heroes, a symbol of heaven.

THE BATTLE OF BUNKER HILL

On June seventeenth, in " seventy-five,"
Old Boston's streets were all alive
　　With those who, waking, heard the gun
　　That first was fired at Lexington.

Old men and matrons thronged the street
With gallant youths and maidens sweet,
    And all the children too were there,
    With rosy cheeks and golden hair,
Gay mingling with the shouting throng
That cheered the soldiery along
    Old Boston's narrow, winding street,
    In rhythm to the drum that beat
And clarion fife that flung afar
The bold, defiant strains of war;
    For every settlement and town
    From all the colonies around
Had sent its band of minute men
To fight the hated red-coat then.
    Like to a day of perfect peace
    That morning's sun illumed the east,
Far out upon the tranquil bay
Flung wide the golden gates of day
    And hurled its shafts of rosy light
    Against the legions of the night;
And June looked down with happy eyes
From out the azure of her skies,
    And nature smiled from field and wood —
    Alas! to stain such scenes with blood.

When General Howe that morning bent
His gaze upon the hill intent,
    His swarthy visage wore a frown;
    He brought his clinched fist fiercely down

Upon the vessel's rail, and swore
That e'er the breaking day was o'er
   He'd blow the rebel works in air
   And float the British ensign there.
Within the town, on roofs and towers,
An anxious throng since early hours
   Had eager watched the new made fort
   And fearful scanned the ships in port.
All through the morn, with irate will,
The cannon thundered at the hill;
   They wreathed the vessels in their smoke
   And hard and bitter words they spoke;
But half their shots flew wide the mark
And others sank in sand and rock,
   So scarce a dozen men were harmed,
   Though long and fierce the frigates stormed.

But when the noon-day sun looked down
Upon the harbor and the town,
   He saw a score of loaded boats,
   Red with the Britons' crimson coats,
Pulled by the sturdy British oar
Up to the hostile Charlestown shore.

   They formed their men in solid ranks,
   And slow advanced upon the banks
Where cowering low, the rebels lay,
In doubt and fear, an easy prey;

Yet paused half way to fire a volley,
To show the traitor horde its folly.
But from the hill came no report,
And all was silence in the fort.
Now, scarce two hundred feet between,
Bnt not a patriot gun is seen.
What! cowers the free-born English heart
At tyranny without a shot?
But look! the flame, the cloud, the rent!
The peal that lifts the firmament,
As darker grows the cloud and higher
Leaps the fierce avenging fire!
But now it is so dense and dark,
We see not friend or foe — but hark!
The fight is o'er, we hear no gun —
O, heaven grant that we have won.

The darksome curtain slowly lifts
And shows the red-coats piled in drifts
Adown the hillside to the shore
In mangled heaps and drenched with gore;
The rest in wild confusion stand
About their boats upon the sand.
But see! they form in line again
And swift advance upon our men.
With straining eyes and bated breath
We watch the pageantry of death,
The swift advance, the earthy mound,
And wait to hear the dreaded sound.

Two hundred feet away at last—
The anxious heart beats hard and fast.
The British fire, but no report
Makes answer from the silent fort.
One hundred feet away, and still
No thunder from the frowning hill.
A flash! a flame! a cloud rolls high,
And scores of red-coat heroes lie
In windrows piled upon the ground
In mingled life and death around.
The rest are huddled on the beach
Beyond the patriots' muskets reach.
'Tis o'er! they will not come again
To "beard the lion in his den."
But look! their line is forming o'er,
With bayonets set they charge once more,
Determined that the foe shall feel
The thirsty point of British steel.
Where are the guns that spoke before
And drenched the hillside red with gore?
Only a scattered few are heard
And scarce the Briton's line is stirred,
And like a mighty wave the rank
Sweeps up the hill and o'er the bank.

Their powder spent, with bar and spade
And musket butt, the patriots made
A stubborn fight to keep them out,
Yet lacked the skill and fled in rout,

And like a helpless, storm-tossed wreck
Swept down the hill and o'er the neck;
Across the isthmus where the blight
Of cannon shot fell left and right,
    And from each crowded roof and spire
    Went up a groan prolonged and dire.
Ah! do not call this fight defeat,
A victory oft crowns retreat.
    'Tis not the battle lost or won,
    It is the deed that they have done.
That they have dared to do this thing
Against a kingdom and a king
    Is in itself a victory
    That shall resound from sea to sea;
A host shall rise when they shall hear
How these have fought and perished here,
    And tyranny shall smitten lie
    Because these men have dared to die;
And not one atom of the cost
In human life shall e'er be lost.
    The birds will tell it to the breeze,
    And it will waft it o'er the seas;
In every land, in every tongue,
Where freedom's songs are joyous sung,
    Fair eyes will flash and brave hearts thrill
    To hear the tale of Bunker Hill.

POEMS OF LOVE

THE GIPSY LASS

Know you the song of the gipsy lass,
  The wandering brunette?
I'm sure you ne'er could have seen her pass,
  Or you would not forget.

About her waist is a gorgeous scarf
  Of crimson and of gold,
As light and free as the gipsy's laugh
  Is every careless fold.

The wind and the sun have tanned her cheek
  And warmed its olive skin,
You look in vain for a feature weak
  In nose, or mouth, or chin.

Her lips are full and a luscious red,
  Her eyes have a dazzled ray,
And if their light on your path is shed
  'Twill steal your heart away.

Know you the song of the gipsy girl,
  A song of love or war?
Of a distant knight in the battle's whirl,
  Or a sighing troubadour.

When she sings of war then her temples burn
  Like the brow of a cavalier,
Her dark eyes flash, and her face grows stern,
  Her voice rings loud and clear.

Her eyes are soft when she sings of love,
    Her blushes come and go,
And you see the night with the stars above,
    And feel the cool winds blow.

O! the dark brunette has a smile for all,
    A lover new each day,
She picks them up, then she lets them fall,
    And flings their hearts away.

Know you the life of the gipsy maid,
    Its sorrow and its grief?
She makes her bed in the green wood's shade,
    Or sleeps on the fragrant heath.

The evening star is her chamber light,
    Her lullaby the streams,
And the restless wind at the dead of night
    Comes moaning in her dreams.

But the lark will sing in the morning hours,
    When night and sleep are through,
To wake the child of the fields and flowers,
    The sunlight and the dew.

SUNSHINE AND SHADOW

Fair are the skies that bend to meet the hills,
Soft are the winds that stir the meadow grass,
Cool is their touch, and fragrant as they pass

With sweet perfumes that come as nature wills;
By floral walks the busy bee distills
His winter store, and sweet wild songsters mass,
While in my glad young heart there is, alas,
Not room to hold the joy that bounds and thrills
When with me 'neath these boughs my lady
    stands.
No other time wears earth so fair a guise
As when I gaze into her dreamy eyes
And read the tale I treasure more than lands,
Or hear her softly breathe her love once more,—
But what if death should snatch her from my
    door?

THINE EYES

'Tis vain to sing the glory of thine eyes—
    Those merry eyes that dance and make us
        glad,
    Those mournful eyes that glance and make us
        sad,
Those liquid depths of laughter and surprise
Where every shade of sweet expression lies;
    Those tearful eyes where pearly dewdrops
        shine,
    Those sunny eyes of radiance divine,
Are more to me than aught in paradise;
For when my heart is heavy with despair
I turn away from all this world of care

And gaze into their depths—then sorrow flees
And joy returns, for hidden there I see
The wondrous light of all thy love for me.
    Divinest eyes! Whence are your mysteries?

LOVE'S INDEX

You may live for sterner duty,
    And may hold yourself apart,
But you cannot hide the beauty
    Of the joy that's in your heart;
For the face reveals the glory
    Of a passion strong and fair,
And love has no hidden story
    But will leave its imprint there.

PEBBLES AND SHELLS

WHEN THOU ART NEAR

When thou art near it matters not to me
What fortune moves the hand of destiny;
I hold it more than wealth, or power, or fame,
To hold thee close and breathe thy dulcet name.

WE TWO

We two, love, stood beside the placid stream,
I saw your face like to a happy dream;
And then a stone slid from the slippery bank,
And silently the angel vision sank.

THE HEART MUST LEAD

The heart must lead along life's doubtful way
    When 'tis too dark for reason's feeble sight;
And if thou heed'st its warnings, day by day,
    In deepest gloom 'twill lead thy steps aright.

A CARESS

Ambition, where are all thy glories now—
    The wealth, the fame, that thou did'st crave
        of yore ?
I'd rather feel her hand upon my brow
    Than any crown that monarch ever wore.

WATCHING AND WAITING

I love my silent watch to keep
Beside the river wide and deep,
  To sit beneath the shady hill
  When all the wood is hushed and still,
And watch the gentle ebb and flow
That dances in the vale below.

I love to hear the waters roar
As down the steep they madly pour,
  Or catch their softer melody
  Upon the breezes wild and free,
When wearily the river's breast
Smooths out its folds in tranquil rest.

I love to watch the silver light
Beneath the mantle of the night,
  When, rich and mellow over all,
  A flood of dancing moonbeams fall,
And every meteor and star
Is blazing in its realm afar.

In love's sweet season, in this shade
Long years ago I wooed a maid;
  A maiden fair as any flower
  That ever bloomed in Eden's bower,
And two young hearts beat tenderly,
Beside the river on the lea.

A cottage stands in yonder dell
Where one fleet year we two did dwell;
　And life was happy as a dream,
　And peaceful as the silver stream,
Until one day, beside the deep
My little darling fell asleep.

I called her long—I called her wild!
But cold in death she only smiled;
　I clasped her hand and bade her wake,
　I told her that my heart would break,
But cold in death her hand was chill,
Her ashen lips were mute and still.

'Twas long ago, that mournful day,
When tenderly we laid away
　The fairest flower in all the vale,
　All cold and lifeless fair and pale.
Folded her hands upon her breast
And gently laid her down to rest.

And now at fall of eventide
I wander by the riverside
　And sit me down beneath the tree
　That sheltered little Nell and me,
And by the river wide and deep
I calmly sit and wait for sleep.

And o'er the crag the waters break
And still my darling will not wake,

And through the mead the river creeps
And still sweet Nellie gently sleeps.
And o'er her grave the willow weeps,
And still my darling sleeps and sleeps.

TO MY LADY SLEEPING

How fair, how tranquil is my lady's pose —
Upon her pillow, wrapped in peaceful dreams,
Hardly a thing of earth or life she seems,
Her lips half parted like a budding rose;
And o'er her couch one golden ringlet flows,
The rest across her pillow wildly streams,
And in the silver moonlight glints and gleams
Like evening sunlight on eternal snows;
And with each breath that softly comes and goes
I see the hand upon her virgin breast
Rise quickly up then slowly sink to rest —
And now she smiles in innocent repose —
O! tell me stars, or wind that softly blows,
Is it for me that smile like heaven glows?

THERE IS BEAUTY

There is beauty without stature,
    In the perfect Grecian mold,
There is beauty without feature
    In the classic dies of old;

There is beauty without fashion,
  There is beauty without art
In the pure and simple passion
  Of a tender loving heart.

Be the passion love or pity,
  Crowned with honor or with shame,
For a dreamland or a city
  Still the lesson is the same;
For the spirit is immortal
  And it shineth through the clay,
Like the sunlight through the portal
  Of a dark and sombre day.

A BOUTONNIERE

It is not that the flower is rare,
Because 'tis bright to see,
But that thy fingers placed it there,
Upon my coat for me;
For at thy touch the ugly tare
Would turn anemone.

ONLY A SLENDER GRAVEN BAND

Only a slender graven band,
  A tiny thing of gold,
I took it from my dead Love's hand
  Her hand so white and cold.

I hid it in my aching breast,
   O! cruel cruel fate,
It filled my heart with mad unrest
   And crushed me with its weight.

I hid it in a secret drawer,
   Away from mortal eye,
But still it drew me by its power —
   I could not let it lie.

I gave it to a distant friend
   To keep for me, alack!
Before he reached his journey's end
   I was upon his track.

I tore it fiercely from his hand
   And threw it in the sea,
Then lay me down upon the sand
   And wept it bitterly.

It fell upon a sea-weed bright
   That floated to the shore,
I seized my treasure with delight
   And kissed it o'er and o'er.

And now I wear it on my hand
   Where all the world may see,—
But only God can understand
   How much it means to me.

TO A WATCH

Thing of beauty, made for duty,
  Ever ticking without rest,
Thou art sleeping in good keeping
  On a peerless maiden's breast,
Thou art nearest to her dearest
  Hopes and longings all unguessed.

O discover if another
  Of her graces is possessed.
For her favor would forever
  Make me dearly doubly blessed,
And no burden e'er would sadden
  If her love I once possessed.

INDIRECTION

Thou may'st not ever lift thy voice in song,
But since my life has seen and felt and known
The height and depth and purpose of thine own,
One poet's verse shall be more deep, more strong.

THE TALKING DAISY

Only a daisy growing by the walk —
Who ever heard a little daisy talk?
I picked the flower and sent it o'er the sea,
And soon it brought my lost love back to me.

THY SMILE

Oh let me linger love awhile,
    A little in the sunshine stay,
The gentle sunlight of thy smile
    That turns my darkest night to day.

LOVE IS A BIRD

Love is a bird that fears the haunts of men,
But seeks instead some sweet secluded glen;
Afar from wealth with peace upon its wings,
Beside the cotter's door he sweetly sings.

I LOVED THEE SO

My life was like a barren, wind-swept plain,
  Surmounted by a brazen, cloudless sky,
  Without an oasis to cheer the eye,
Or e'en a shrub to tell of cooling rain;
Then to my heart all feverish with pain,
  Came love with dewy wings, and told of thy
  Sweet face, thy blush, thy melancholy sigh,
And of thy soul so pure and free from stain.
  Then straightway all the barren waste of years
  Was flooded by a shower of happy tears
And in that hour my soul forgot its woe;
  New pleasures filled with joy the glad old
    earth,
  New hopes and longing taught my soul the
    worth
Of life, and all because I loved thee so.

ONE MEMORY

Though sun and moon and stars should pale,
And all my earthly friends should fail,
  If I could keep Thee in my heart
  Unsullied, from the world apart;
This one great joy amid life's woe
Would make my cup to overflow.

PYGMALION TO GALATEA

O soulless Galatea! Thou art stone,
And yet my hands have given to thy form
A grace that never yet was seen of flesh,
And to thy brow a beauty never born.
But no — my throbbing heart and fevered brain
Ne'er held so fair a dream of womanhood;
My trembling hands but freed thee from the cold,
Relentless stone that held thy matchless form,
And thou didst live in some forgotten age
When men were gods and women were their
    queens.

O peerless Galatea! Thou art free,
And I have wrought that rich deliverance.
What wild, ecstatic joy it was to see
Thy goddess features grow from out the stone,
As year by year I labored slowly on.
And, as I worked, it seemed thy noble face
Grew warm beneath my touch; I thought thy
    lips
Would surely speak when I had set them free;
But when I pressed them with my own, the twain
Were hard and cold and passionless as death.

O heartless Galatea! Speak to me,
Though thou canst say but cold and cruel words;
For I would see thee move thy speechless lips
E'en though their breath did freeze my very soul.

I cannot bear to look upon thy face
Its cold indifference would break my heart,
And drive me mad.   I cannot bear to hold
Thy senseless hand, its lifeless touch is like
The hand of death.   Oh! give one simple sign
Of life and love and I will rest content!

O dearest Galatea!   Live for me
And I will crown thy life with priceless love.
My watchful tenderness shall soothe thy pain
And shield thee from all sorrow and distress,
My boundless love shall be thy refuge and
Thy strength and I will live to give thee joy.
If love be dead and cold within thy breast,
Mine own warm heart shall kindle it anew
Into a flame that shall transcend the skies,
And live though all things else in life shall fail.

O senseless Galatea!   Thou art dead!
And yet, I swear thy soul shall come again.
Such love as mine would start the blood within
Thy pulseless breast, and call thy spirit back,
Though death had claimed it for a thousand
      years.
My heart shall beat in mute appeal for thee,
Each breath my lips shall cry aloud for thee,
And all my life shall be a living prayer
Unto the gods for thy deliverance;
And I will watch, and wait, and pray, till heaven

Shall give thee back to earth, or death shall loose
My cruel chains and let me go to thee.

A NEW–BLOWN ROSE

Dew-gemmed, sun-kissed and reaching towards
    the light,
  Op'ning its folds, soft tinted, red and rare,
  Breathing its fragrance on the morning air,
'Tis just the rose to give my love delight,
I'll pick it now, and give it her to-night.
  But 'tis so sweet, so fragrant and so fair,
  Smiling, blushing upon the rose bush there,
I cannot pluck it from the stem to blight
  E'en though it be for my dear love to wear.

THE POET'S LOVE

The poet's love should be a maid so fair
That all would pause in pleasure and surprise,
Whene'er she passed, to feast their hungry eyes
Upon a sight so beautiful and rare.
The poet's love should have a mind and dare
To criticise her minstrel's faulty song,
To tell him where the feeble lines went wrong,
And then to praise the little beauty there.
The poet's love should be a maid of prayer
And draw her knowledge of the lyric art

Out of the longings of her woman's heart,
With eyes to see and heart to truly care
For peerless truth, then while the poet sings
She lifts him up to higher nobler things.

SWEET SMILING LIPS

Sweet smiling lips, so wan and white,
That yester morn were laughing light
Oh! tell me has her spirit fled,
Or does my loved one sleep instead?
Oh! will she wake with morning bright,
Sweet smiling lips?

But one brief day has taken flight,
Since love redeemed its holy plight
But now all happiness has sped,
Sweet smiling lips.

Yet yesterday when we were wed
I thought the simple words you said
Were something Time could never blight;
But now that dream has vanished quite.
Oh! come back flushing, blushing red
And tell me that she is not dead,
Sweet smiling lips.

LOVE OR GOLD

Gold is a stingy offering
  In sorrow's raging storm,
It cannot consolation bring —
  But love is deep and warm.

Love's bright and holy tributes spring
  From hearts with love aglow,
While all gold's favors hollow ring
  As empty idle show.

THE ROSE AND THE THORN

I sought the flower I loved the best
  Amid the garden's varied bloom,
  A perfect bud with sweet perfume,
A rose more fair than all the rest
That I might wear it on my breast
  And guard it ever tenderly.
  I found the flower that bloomed for me
Beside the pathway, smiling lest
  The wanderer might pass it by
  And it be left to fade and die.
I seized the flower with wild delight,
  Though cruelly my hand was torn.
It faded e'er another night
  And left me but the ugly thorn.

AT DEVOTION

Now kneels my lady at her couch in prayer,
Her two white hands uplifted to the skies,
To ask of Him beneficent and wise
Another night of tender love and care.
And as I watch my lady kneeling there
With deep devotion in her tender eyes,
While from her lips fair phrased petitions rise,
Her robe like to the garb that angels wear,
But made the whiter by her streaming hair;
I deem that from the gates of Paradise
An angel heard my heart's impatient cries
For woman's love, and answered then and there.
Fair angel say one word of grace for me
For God must surely hear and answer thee.

BOATING ON THE LAKE

The stars are bright, the moon is high,
    And night winds whisper on the shore.
    Our boat is slowly gliding o'er
A lake as placid as the sky,
Where moon and stars reflected lie.
    The liquid laughter of Lenore,
    The gentle dipping of her oar
Awake a happy lullaby.
"Ah! lady fair," I musing said,
    "If life is but a boat like this,

With you to row and me to kiss,
What joy 'twould be when we are wed!"
"'Ah, no," she said —"''Tis very clear
That you will row and I shall steer."

PLAYING TENNIS

The winds are playing with her hair,
  Her cheeks are flushing like the rose,
She stands with racket raised in air,
  To catch the ball that comes and goes.
She springs more fleetly than the roe
  And serves with swift unerring flight,
Like willows when the breezes blow
  She bends, and sways, and turns, and light
Upon the lawn her footfalls pass,
As thistledown upon the grass.
  Three brilliants brought from Afric's strand
Reflect the morning's rosy light,
And yet her eyes are twice as bright
  As all the jewels on her hand.

YES OR NO

They sat within a dreamy bower,
  And passed the hours in converse sweet;
  He by her side, yet at her feet,
Nor heard the clock upon the tower
That chimed each swiftly passing hour;

And in each moment passing fleet
He racked his wits for some conceit
To supplement his feeble power
   In asking for the maiden's hand;
While she impatient of delay,
But looked the words she dared not say,
   And wished that he might understand.
Only a word and idle breath,
But yes was life, and no was death.

IF I BUT HAD THE KEY

If I but had the little key
   That opes my lady's wayward heart
I'd turn the bolt, and then I'd see
   If love e'er pierced it with his dart;
And if her love was all for me
   I'd enter in and lock the door,
   And live with love forevermore.

THE BALL DRESS

They dressed my lady for the ball —
   In softest satins, fashioned so
   They left her arms and neck to show
That they were fair as snows that fall,
With richest laces over all.
   About her form's exquisite mould
   Fell many a graceful shining fold,

And admiration filled the hall.
  But where's the beauty of a dress
  To match this lady's loveliness?
Her sweet address, her happy mien,
  That glossy hair, those eyes of brown,
  That sunny face that ne'er could frown,
Would grace the raiment of a queen.

THE FISHER-MAIDEN

Her smile is like the morning bright
  When shines the glorious sun,
Her eyes are like the flashing light
  From out the diamond stone.

Her lips are like the cherry red —
  They hide such teeth of pearl,
And when by laughter they are spread
  There's such a tempting curl.

Faint blushes play upon her cheeks,
  Like ripples on the Nile,
I'd like to catch one as it streaks
  From dimple into smile.

I love her well and told her so
  When we were out to-day,—
She answered me so soft and low
  And did not say me nay.

A PORTRAIT OF MY LADY

O words! weak words, how can I give thee form
And color like the fair young face I fain
Would paint?   How can I give thee light and
    shade,
And strength and truth and gentle earnestness,
And crown them all with that rich coronet
Of human life, a great and noble soul?

O eyes! deep lucent pools of tenderness
And truth, where all that fair or good in earth
Or heaven mirrored lies, where burns the fire
Of proud ambition towards the infinite,
And soul that will not rest content with small
Uncertain things, but needs must climb from
    height
To height, undazzled by the altitude,
That cannot rest until it knoweth God,
The source, and author of the universe,
The fountain of all beauty and all truth,
And knowing Him—must love the mystery
Of earth, of air, of sun, of sky, and all
That moves and lives in this great universe.
O eyes, so strong, so deep, so grave, so full
Of that unspoken language of the soul;
Mine own poor orbs go down before thy gaze
As 'twere an angel sent to me from heaven

To read my heart and pierce my inmost soul;
So rare, so pure, so heavenly is your light.

O lips! fair servants of the heart and brain,
Expressing all her thoughts and feelings in
Such myriad forms of speech, and diverse looks,
And little intonations quaint and sweet
That saying nothing, mean a volume full,
And fill the poet's heart with joy and fear;
That in their speech let fall such pearls of truth,
Such spotless gems of fancy and of wit,
It seemed she held the chalice of all wit.
All wisdom, and all fancy in her hands,
And did but lavish forth what pleased her mood,
And in such tones it seemed a siren spake;
And who shall paint the rapture of those lips
When through their ruby depths there breaks a
        smile
Like sunlight through the rosy gates of morn,
Or like a primrose parted by a sunbeam.
O lips of beauty, strength and eloquence,
Of tenderness and power all blent in one,
O bless me with one word of gracious praise,
Of commendation for this poor attempt,
And more — O ecstacy too great for words,
One word of love, of sweet abiding love,
Beside which all life's other gold is dross.

O face! the looking glass of woman's soul,
The full blown rose of all her sweet perfection,

The never failing index of the heart,
What strength, what beauty in thy every line,
What high-born thought, what thrilling passion
    speaks
In eye, in mouth, and in thy noble brow;
What envy for the rose is in thy blush,
What venom for the lily in thy skin.
O face, what greater rapture could man know
Than biding near her while my lady dreams,
And watch the play, the change of light and
    shade,
Upon her face, when life's full chord is struck
And flesh reveals the spirit that's within.

O form! that matches symmetry with grace,
And eloquence and brawn, with beauty too,
Where is the Venus, born of ancient art,
Or Diana, so strong and swift of foot,
In noble bust that can compare with thee?
How flows the rich profusion of thy hair
In glossy tresses down a lily neck,
How swells the contour of thy virgin breast
With all that is most noble in the heart,
What graceful curves thy sloping shoulders make,
And how above the rest, serene and full
Thy noble forehead speaks intelligence.

O queen of beauty! regent of my heart!
I bring this poor portrayal of thy grace,

A better theme for Petrarch, or the bard
Who tuned his lyre for goddesses of old,
And beg thee hang it in thy banquet hall,
Not that it is sufficient in itself,
But that it is a labor of such love.
There let it hang, upon the frescoed wall
Just where some merry sunbeam deigns to slant,
Itself a sunbeam from the source of light,
That some may know, who pause and chance to
    look
Above the mould, and cobwebs at their feet,
That some poor fool has dreamed, and e'en
    aspired
Out of his boundless love that gave him strength,
To paint for man, that fairest work of God,
Set like a jewel in a grosser world
That better shows it forth, a perfect woman.

POEMS OF CHILDHOOD

ALL ABOUT FROGS

A frog is something like a toad,
Only he lives down by the road
Where there's a pond and lily pads,
And toads, they live in folk's back yards.

A toad is fat, a frog is lean,
The suit he wears is always green,
Except his vest, and that is yellow,
And he's a mighty funny fellow.

Sometimes he sits beside a pad
And smiles at you, like he was glad,
And then he goes down in kerplunk,
And kicks around like he was drunk;

And when you think he's surely drowned,
He's gone so long, you look around
And you will see him on a stone,
A catchin' flies and havin' fun.

Sometimes I poke him with a stick
To see him jump, he goes so quick,
So very quick, I do declare
You cannot see him in the air.

But some bad boys throw stones at him.
And he gets killed, if he don't swim
Down out of sight, and quiet stay
Until the bad boys go away.

My pa, he knows, and he says frogs
Are but big grown up pollywogs;
I didn't see how that could be,
And so I thought one day I'd see.

I went and caught a pollywog
And laid him down upon a log,
And watched him for an hour or so,
But I am sure he didn't grow.

When I told Papa, he looked queer
And said it took almost a year
For them to grow, and that was why
I could not see it with my eye.

SHADOWS

A little tree my hand could reach around,
Can cast a mighty shadow on the ground;
So little folks if they are cross at play,
May make dark shadows chase the sun away.

HOW TOMMY WALKED ON THE WATER

Last Friday afternoon when school was done
And Tommy 'n' me were looking out for fun,
A new idea came into Tommy's head
While we were sitting by Ma's posy bed.

"I'm goin' to do a miracle for you,"
He said, "If you won't tell, honest and true,"
And then he went into the wagon shed
And got two bladders bigger than my head.

And then we went down to the old red mill,
Where there's a pond, with water in it still,
And Tommy got upon a log of wood
And crawled out on it careful as he could.

And then he fished his pockets for some strings,
And on his big toes tied them bladder things,
Then said he'd show me how that Peter done,
And do a miracle and have some fun.

He stepped right off just like the pond was
    ground,
With both his feet a-bobbin' all around,
Without a thought of his new pair of clothes
And went head first right down upon his nose.

His head went down like it was made of lead
And both his feet came up in sight instead;
'Twas like a fly a-walkin' on the ceilin',
I saw him kick but couldn't hear him squealin'.

And all the time he tried to reach his toes
And break them strings, a-standin' on his nose;
But I got scat when he had kicked a spell,
And hollered fire as tight as I could yell.

Then Pa came runnin' out without his hat
And in his stocking feet, a-lookin' scat;
We got poor Tommy out and home in bed,
A-lookin' pale and white, and almost dead.

And Ma she cried and kissed him lots and said,
" It was a mercy that he wasn't dead;"
And Pa he said that he would tend to me
And give me something pleasant after tea.

THE BUTTERCUP

Dear little chalice, catching the sunlight,
Holding the drops of the morning dew,
Growing so sweetly here by the roadside,
Would I might learn a lesson from you.
Out of the sunlight and glory of God,
To gather the sweetness and leave the rue.

ALL ABOUT GIRLS

A girl is something with a braid,
That wears an apron and is 'fraid;
And women, they are grown up girls,
With longer hair and lots more curls.

I have a sister 'n' her name's Nan,
And she can't ever be a man,
Or run about upon the hay
And have a jolly time at play.

All she can do is have a doll
And take it out with her to call,
Or pick some flowers and make bouquets,
Which are the dullest kind of plays.

Girls have to stay inside the house
And keep as quiet as a mouse,
But boys can go outside and yell,
And when they're tired, come in a spell.

Girls have to wash the dishes too,
And sweep the room when that is through,
While boys go off to slide and skate
And don't get home till it is late.

But girls are good for little things,
Like mending balls, or tying strings,
And sometimes Nan will help a feller
When he has lost his ball down cellar.

There's one thing girls don't have to do,
That's get in wood, like me or you,
And if they did I know they'd cry
And then not pile the wood up high.

But Nan, she's better than the others,
For she is good to both her brothers,
And I am sure she'd like to be
A boy like Tommy or like me.

ALL ABOUT BOYS

A boy is something that makes noise
And smashes things and loses toys,—
That is until they're grown up, then
Folks do not call them boys, but men.

The things boys like the best are bad
Or things that make their mothers' sad,
Like going on the pond to skate
When 'tis not safe, and stayin' late.

Most boys don't care so much for dolls —
The things they like are bats and balls
And circuses and kinds of play
Where there's a horse that runs away.

Small boys are always full of tricks,
Like tickling you with straws and sticks,
Or putting on some furs to wear
And fright'ning you a playing bear.

My youngest brother's name is Jack —
Sometimes he takes me on his back
Just like a horse and gallops round
And then he spills me on the ground.

My brother Tommy says that girls
Ain't good for much but raisin' curls,
And that folks keep them just for hair
To stuff the parlor rocking chair.

And then he says it's only play
And they don't mean all that they say,
And when he's grown up to a man
He'll buy fine things for little Nan.

PLAYING HOUSE

There is a play, I guess you wish you knew it,
And I will tell you just the way to do it,
If you won't tell — that is, not every one
For 'tis a secret and such jolly fun.

You get your Pa to go down to the store
And get a box big as the parlor door,
And then you have him put it on the ground
Where there is grass and shade trees all around.

And then you tease your Papa more and more
Until he gets a saw and makes a door
Low down upon one side where doors should be,
And then 'tis ready for the family.

The family is Tommy, Jack and I,
When they will play, and also Butterfly
When she's around, (she really is a cat)
But in our play a dog upon the mat.

I'm mistress of the house and bake the bread
And do such things, and Tommy's uncle Ned

He says that's so that he can sit up late
And not be sent to bed when it is eight.

Jack plays that he is Pa, and goes away
To Boston, so that he can stay all day;
At night when he comes home to Tommy 'n' me
He tells about the things he's been to see.

To make it night you spread your mother's shawl
Over the door till you can't see at all;
Then go to bed, but Tommy says he dreams
Which is not nice for then he kicks and screams.

When you get tired of this, you wake and say,
" I guess it must be getting almost day,"
And then you look out doors and it is light
And so you give up playing it is night.

And when you've played at having dolly sick
And sending for the Doctor very quick,
And had a washing day and ironing too,
And many other things that you may do

A bell will ring and then it is you'll know
How quick this play will make the minutes go,
And you will run into the house and see
What good things your Mamma has got for tea.

HOW SANTA CLAUS CAME DOWN THE
CHIMNEY

Last Christmas eve, when we were snug in bed,
And all the lights were out, Tommy, he said,
" I'd like to know how 'tis, with pack and all,
That Santa Claus gets down the chimney hole."

" Let's lay awake and see and then we'll know;
Won't it be fun to see him squeezed up so?"
And so we laid awake, but by and by,
I got to sleeping some with my left eye.

But still I saw the chimney with my right,
And by and by there came the queerest sight,
A little man no bigger than Tom Thumb,
With a little pack no bigger than my drum

Came sliding down the chimney more and
    more,
Until he went kerbump upon the floor;
And then he looked around the room a spell,
But very soon his pack began to swell.

It kept a swelling, more and more and more,
Till it was bigger than the parlor door;
And then I saw that it was full of toys
And books and dolls, and things for girls and
    boys.

And soon the little man had grown so tall
He didn't seem to be a dwarf at all;
And then he took some things out of his pack
And filled my stocking till I thought 'twould
    crack.

And then the pack grew small, and small and
    small,
Until it wasn't bigger 'n' nothin' 'tall,
And Santa Claus he was a dwarf once more,
And climbed up back as he had come before.

Then just as Santa Claus got out of sight
I opened my left eye and it was light,
And there were all the things for Tommy 'n' me,
A-bursting out just as I knew they'd be.

But when I told him, Tommy laughed, and said,
I was a foolish little sleepy head,
But by and by, he said, "It must be so,
For Santa Claus had left the things, you know."

A WISH

I wish that Pa was Santa Claus
With reindeer and a pack, because,
Then he would have such lots of toys
For all his little girls and boys.

Then every day would Christmas be
With lots of fun for Tommy 'n' me,
We'd hang our stockings every night
And Pa would fill them 'fore 'twas light.

Then when I'd grow'd to be a man,
Just as my mother says I can,
I would be Santa Claus like him
And fill boys' stockings to the brim.

THE SUNBEAM AND THE SHADOW

A sunbeam from the source of light
Came flashing down to earth,
His face was fair, his eyes were bright,
His heart was full of mirth.

Right joyfully the sunbeam came
To swell the perfect day,
Yet where he fell, it was a shame,
Dark shadows round him lay.

" Why come you here? " a shadow cried,
And on him darkly frowned,
" This is our only place to hide
For many miles around."

" I come to cheer each lonely place
And turn the dark to day,

137

To light a smile on sorrow's face
And drive its gloom away."

" Poor foolish thing," the shadow said,
" Earth is no place for day,
Her life is dark and cold and dread,
You know not what you say.

" I cover up its want and woe
And wrap the earth in sleep,
That none may see and none may know
What countless millions weep."

The merry little sunbeam laughed,
" That is not right," he said,
" I've seen the smart of sorrow's shaft,
I dry their tears instead.

Earth hath her sorrows and her joys,
Her sunshine and her rain,
But love is worth all life's alloys,
Its pleasure worth its pain."

And then the sunbeam shone so bright
Upon his happy way,
He pierced the shadow with his light
And frightened him away.

CONFESSIONS OF A STREET GAMIN

Well governor you do look slick,
But yer can't give me guff;
I guess you think I be a fool,
Or not quite up to snuff?

Yer really want ter know, yer say,
What we street duffers do?
Gosh! if yer ain't the queerest cud
I ever had to chew.

Yer want ter put it in a book
That yer a-goin' to sell?
Well governor, yer welcome to't,
But there ain't much ter tell.

Me dad he was a gintleman,
A-keepin' of a bar,
Before he got ter swillin' so,—
I never hed no ma.

But one dark night he got so bad
I had to take a sneak,
An' while he was a chasin' me
He fell inter the creek.

I s'pose you'll think 'twas mighty queer
I blubbered an' felt bad,
Yer see I had ter love him some —
Yer know he was me dad.

But by-and-by I got a pal,—
Why, don't yer know, a pard?—
When I was down upon me luck
An' things went mighty hard,

He helped me if he had the swag,
He alluz was a brick;
But pretty soon there came a time
That made me mighty sick.

One day we two wuz tossin' cops
Upon a pavin' stun,
When up the street there came a cab,
The hosses on the run.

And right in front uv that durned team,
A runnin' fit ter drop,
Was jest the purtiest little gal,
It made me knocker stop.

But Jim he jumped as quick as whiz
An' snatched the little girl,
An' then the cab went thund'rin' by,
An' all was in a whirl.

But when I got me senses back —
For somethin' hit me head —
An' looked around for Jim, me pal,
He was a lyin' dead.

I laid right down upon the stones.
An' bellowed side er Jim;
He was the only pal I had
An' I'd er died for him.

Then all the swell folks in the cab
Got out an' stood around,
They all took off their hats to Jim.
A lyin' on the ground.

There was a lady in the crowd
Dressed up alfired grand,
With silk an' lace upon her togs
An' rings upon her hand.

She went right up ter my poor pard,.
An' then knelt down by him,
An' held his head upon her arm;
That's jest like some them wim.

She looked so mighty beaut' an' good,.
A strokin' cully's head,
Her eyes they were so sorrowful,
I wished 'twas me that's dead.

I know I'd been a better chap
If I had had a ma,
Or some one good ter talk ter me,.
An' look at me like her.

She said it warn't so bad ter die
If we but loved the Farder
He's got a swell place in the sky,
An' He can make us gladder;

She said some day that I might go
And live with that big swell,
But all them preacher duffers say
They know we'll go ter hell.

Well, them air snobs, they did the square
By me an' my poor pal,
They dressed him up in dandy togs
An' made a funeral.

They got a real howler too,
What said that God is love,
An' that he cared as much for Jim
As any other cove.

An' there was posies all round Jim,
He had a bran new suit,
The first un that he ever had,
An' everything was beaut.

An' when the preacher told 'bout Jim,
How 'twas he got the swipe,
I saw most all them dandy swells
A-feelin' for a wipe.

I couldn't blink a wink that night
After I douced the glim,
All I could do was kick about,
An' blubber 'n' think o' Jim,

An' loosin' cully seemed to bust
The luck I'd had a spell,
I couldn't get a trot to do
An' papes they wouldn't sell.

An' then I lost the snuggery
That we hed hed together,
An' so I hed ter bunk out doors
In mighty nippin' weather.

An' when I couldn't find a snug,
I jest walked up an' down ;
The glims they looked so warm an' bright
In houses up in town,

It made me sick to look at um,
An' then I'd go away,
An' walk, an' walk, an' walk, an' walk,
Until it got to day.

Sometimes I'd think uv things I'd heard,
But they wuz mighty dim,
About the gov'ner in the sky
And how folks prayed to him,

An' then I'd ask him for some grub
An' togs ter keep me warm,
An' jest some place ter lay me head
Inside out of the storm;

I didn't ax him for a bed,
But jest some straws, you see,
An' then I'd hark an' try ter hear
If he would answer me.

But all I'd hear was rumblin' wheels,
An' jinglin' horse car bells,
He never cares for such as me,
He goes in for them swells.

About that time I jined the gang,
An' then we bust the bank;
They was a mighty wicked crowd
That cussed an' fit an' drank.

I didn't know how bad they was
Until we made the deal,
An' then they'd carved me quick as wink
Ef I'd a dared ter squeal.

Then next we tried a big stone front
Where there was lots of tin;
Big Devil Dick, he bust a light
An' then he put me in.

I was a-creepin' ter the door,
Ter let the fellers in,
When all at once there was a flash
An' then an awful din.

But when I got me senses back
After the shootin' fuss,
I was down in the hospital,
With such a jolly nuss.

Them was about the bulliest days
That ever I hev hed,
With such good things to stuff an' swill
An' such a dozy bed.

You see the gang had all been tuck
But Dick, an' he lay low,
An' I was sech a little duck
The jedge, he let me go.

An' when I left the hospital,
'Twas mighty hard ter leave,
I was a-lookin limp an' white
An' hed one empty sleeve.

But now the luck all comes my way —
I've got another pard —
For folks is mighty good ter me
An' times they aint so hard.

An' now sometimes I gets a tip,
A nickel or a dime,
An' sometimes when the biz is dull
I get a little time.

Why don't you know? I am a trot
Down at the new hotel,
It is a mighty shiny place,
An' ev'rything is swell.

You've really been a-chalkin' it?
Well, if yer ain't a cad;
I hope yer've put it rather light,
Then I won't seem so bad.

Day, reditor, I'm much obliged
For such a heap of tin;
But that's the sarvants' gong yer hear
An' I must go ter din.

POEMS OF OLD NEW ENGLAND

THE DESERTED HOMESTEAD

Poor are the pilgrims on life's stony way
Who, turning from the beaten track astray,
To some secluded spot, or quiet roof,
Where once perchance they spent their happy
  youth;
Who ne'er have felt at each familiar turn,
With eyes that fill and hearts that throb and
  burn,
The quiet charms of dear familiar ways.
The half forgotten joys of other days.

How well do I recall that happy day
When turning from the noisy world away
By quiet lanes that never failed to charm,
I sought my home, the old deserted farm.
It was a winsome day in early fall,
A time when nature broodeth over all
Her broad domain of fruitful fields and woods,
And woos the wand'rer in her gayest moods.
I heard the south wind whisper to the corn,
Its pennons streamed and rustled back in scorn;
Each grain field caught the sunbeams in their
  flight
And shot them back in mellow amber light;
In deeper shades the birches' silver sheen
Shed softest rays the emerald boughs between,
The distant hills were robed in gold and dun
And hazy skies subdued the summer sun;

Fair orchards laden with their golden fruit
And gardens rich in bursting pod and root
Diversified the scene, and to my eyes
Seemed like a Peri's dream of Paradise.
The merry harvesters were all a-field,
(Keen are the scythes and sickles that they wield),
With jocund song, the reaper and the mower
Went through the fields and garnered in the store,
While ripe'ning nuts, from tall majestic trees
Came down in showers before the merry breeze,
Gay squirrels scolding frisked from limb to limb
And woke the woods and swelled the harvest
    hymn;
And as I journeyed through that pleasant lane
Where peace and plenty seemed to ever reign,
I thought how sordid is our bitter strife
For gold beside this quiet country life.

But now the dear old homestead comes in sight
Upon the hill above me, on the right,—
Ah! can it be the same, the grand old place,
The mansion on the hill, that oft my face
In childhood's happy days so eager spied,
The home that was our father's joy and pride,
That kin had held two hundred years and more,
Since first the Pilgrims landed on this shore?
Or is it that a flood of blinding tears
And all the growth and change of many years
Have come between me and the dear old scene,

And make my youthful palace seem so mean?'
O gold! that robs this world of half its wealth
O lore! that cheats the soul of joy and health,
I'd blot these weary years from heart and brain
To live that sweet delusion o'er again.
But wherefore mourn, or sigh, or think it strange,.
Earth moves, time flies, man grows and all
    things change.

'Tis clearer now, I see the gable roof
Look outward from the elm-tree's verdant woof
Like some familiar face, and lower still
The friendly wild-rose on the window sill,
Where oft I sat when day and toil were o'er,
And longed to roam the world on sea and shore,
And dreamed of love and fame and cruel wars,
Awhile the night wind whispered to the stars.
Ah yes! I see the woodbine on the ell,
The towering wellsweep that I knew so well,
And on the barn the same old weather-vane
That told of yore of sunshine and of rain.
But half the quaint old roof has fallen in
And winter blasts have worn its shingles thin,
While each dejected window-sash complains
That storms and stones have robbed it of its
    panes;
Upon one hinge the front door grinds and
    squeaks,
Like some poor human thing it plainly speaks

Of sad neglect and summer suns and rains
That make it old and fill its joints with pains.

Here is the ancient fire-place, broad and tall,
How cheerful was its firelight on the wall;
Here oft I sat on stormy winter nights
And watched the restless ever-changing lights
Upon the logs, or traced a tiny spark
Far up the dingy flue into the dark;
'Twas by this stone that grandma used to sit
Upon those winter eves and drowse and knit,
While I would watch the stocking as it grew
And count the stitches while the needles flew,
And seated by the cosy kitchen hearth
We passed the hours in jest and merry laugh
That mocked the fury of the howling storm—
Then came the thought, how dear a place is
     home.

Some prudent squirrel leaves his winter store
Upon the landing of my chamber door,
And rude rats scamper o'er the floor and hide
Behind the dingy walls that were my pride;
For vermin comes to gloat o'er man's decay,
And haunt his home when he has passed away.
But through the broken window dark with mold
I see the dreamy hills I knew of old;
And now it seemeth like a few short hours
Since first I scaled those silent mountain towers.—

Majestic hills! I love thy purple range,
I love thee now, and thou wilt never change.

Here is the barn,— Ah! what a place to play
When mow and loft are filled with new-mown
    hay,
And all the air is sweet with clover scent—
To climb the beams and jump from bent to bent,
Or search the hay-mows for a stolen nest;
Of all the play-rooms known this is the best.
And when I gaze adown yon winding lane,
My age departs and youth comes back again.
I see a barefoot boy in homely dress,
The prince of that rich kingdom, happiness,
A brimless palmleaf is his regal crown,
His ruddy cheeks are tinged with russet brown,
His sunny face could never wear a cloud,
No rich estates could make him half so proud,
His scepter is a leafless maple browse,
His Majesty is driving home the cows.

How peaceful is yon meadows' stretch of green,
In sunset light, the autumn hills between,
Deep down beneath the grass, by reed and rock
The little brook sings to the meadow lark,
Right merrily he sings the livelong day
To cheer the weary farmer with his lay.
What pain would fill his heart if father knew
That witch-grass claimed the fields where clover
    grew,

That all the meadow hay was filled with swale,
His cherished wood-lot stripped for tie and rail,
That all the pasture-lots were choked with brush,
The meadow lowlands grown to reed and rush;
If he could see the ancient orchard's rows
Of stately trees uprooted by the blows
That strip the rotting shingles from the shed
And shake the crazy rafters overhead,
That raze the gates and fences to the ground,
And scatter direst desolation round;
If he could see the gruesome foreign hordes
That gather round our old-time festal boards,
Who swarm upon these farms and till our fields
And turn our ancient looms and spinning-wheels;
A folk who know no law but fire and steel,
Who do not glory in the nation's weal,
Who cannot speak or write our mother tongue,
Who feel no thrill when freedom's songs are sung,
A class who hate all forms of government
And fill this happy land with discontent;
Ah! well for him his humble life was taken
Before New England homesteads were forsaken.

'Tis eventide, the shades of night draw near
And one by one the silent stars appear,
Those silver tapers that the angels hold
Above the clouds to view the sleeping wold,
The night-winds faintly whisper as they pass,
A cricket chirps beside me in the grass,

The elm-tree gently stirs its countless leaves,
And over all a benediction breathes
More deep than sleep, more tranquil than the
    calms
Of some far oasis with breathless palms,—
But hark! upon the air so deep and still
Rude breaks the sound of wheels upon the hill,
The wheels that bear me from this sweet retreat
Back to the city, rife with dust and heat.

Farewell! farewell! fair haven of my youth,
Thou sweet abode of innocence and truth,
And though my feet may leave thee far behind,
No chance or change shall blot thee from my
    mind.
And when at eve the city streets are hot
Fond memory shall lead me to this spot,
Then for the din, the rumble and the grind,
Mine ears shall hear the murmur of the wind;
And when at last life's little day is spent
And death shall claim this form, infirm and bent,
I beg some friend to whom I once was dear,
To break the turf and lay the poet here.
Here 'neath the elm where every idle breath
Shall murmur low a requiem for death,
Where first in spring the lilac sheds its bloom
And last in fall the verdure gathers gloom;
That men may know of all the classic ground
Where poets sleep, the leagued world around,

I place New England high above the rest,
I hold this spot the fairest and the best.

GETTIN' HUM

There air some mighty purty scenes
Ter see upon the farm,
An' there ain't nothin' in the town
Ter my notion ter charm
Yer like those homely kentry scenes,
With all their quiet ways,
Instead o' everything agog,
An' everything ablaze.

I went down ter the city once
Ter see what I could see,
An' got alfired lonesome like
An' blue as I could be;
The folks all look so worried like
An' never stop ter talk,
An' don't say nuthin' 'bout the craps,
An' gallup when they walk.

I didn't see a bit o' grass,
Or any kind o' land,
Or anything but bricks and stun
An' houses built so grand
You'd hardly dast ter look at 'em,
An' made so tarnal high

You'd kinder hev ter hold yer breath
Whenever yer went by.

The furniture is all so soft
Made out o' plush and hair,
It kinder seemed ter say ter you
Sit down on me with care;
I didn't sit down good and hard
The whole time I wuz there —
I tell yer what, I longed sometimes
Fur my ole straight-backed chair.

My cousins were so tarnal p'lite
An' made so many bones
About my comin' down ter town,
An' called me Mr. Jones,
An' axed sech funny questions too,
They made me want ter run,
I'd gin a V ter heard um say
"How be yer, Jonathan."

I shook the dust off o' my feet
When I had stayed a week,
And got out of that Babylon,
Where everything wuz Greek,
An' homes were kept so mighty fine
You'd think they're made for kings,
With beds that wouldn't let yer sleep
For fear you'd bust their springs.

When I gut hum 'twas harvest time
An' there wuz golden corn
A-standin' waitin' in the shocks,
An' mother's dinner horn
Cum ringin' cheery down the road,
It sounded mighty sweet,
It seemed ter say, cum home old man
An' git somethin' ter eat.

An' there wuz cattle in the fields
An' punkins on the vines
An' flaming maples in the woods
Among the spruce an' pines,
An' squirrels jumped from limb to limb
Where there was nuts to spare,
An' autumn's haze wuz on the hills,
An' peace wuz in the air.

An' when I saw our little home
A-nestlin' in the trees,
Jest in the sunshine an' the shade
With jest a bit o' breeze,
I'll 'low my heart swelled up a bit
An' kept a-swellin' more,
Until it fairly bust itself
With Hannah at the door.

An' when she hugged me roun' the neck
An' kissed me on the cheek,

An' said, "how be yer, Jonathan,"
I swow, I couldn't speak.
'Twuz worth a year of city life,
An' more than kingdom come —
'Bout all the fun o' goin' off
Is jest a gettin' hum.

SONG OF THE PLOUGHMAN

Bring forth the plough, the frost is out,
And spring is here without a doubt;
Upon the cattle put their yoke,
The field and fallow must be broke,
For he who reaps in harvesting
Must sow his seeds in early spring.

The plough is brought from loft or shed,
And forth the sturdy steers are led,
The yoke is placed upon their necks,
The plough is scoured all free from specks,
Then Sam, the plough boy, whip in hand,
Beside the cattle takes his stand.

Turn, turn, turn, empty are crib and bin,
Turn, turn, turn, ploughing the daisies in,
Turn, turn, turn, breaking the tufted sward,
Turn, turn, turn, reaping a rich reward.

The patient cattle plod along,
Their necks are bent, the yoke is strong;
The gleaming plough-share cleaves the earth,
The burning sunbeams dance in mirth,
And oft the farmer stops the plough
And wipes the sweat from off his brow.

At every turn the plough-boy's "Gee,"
Across the field makes melody,
Full well the cattle know his whip,
They oft have felt its stinging tip,
Yet spite of muzzles as they pass,
They stop to nip the tender grass.

Turn, turn, turn, empty are crib and bin,
Turn, turn, turn, ploughing the daisies in,
Turn, turn, turn, breaking the tufted sward,
Turn, turn, turn, reaping a rich reward.

The robin greets the farmers' toil
With notes of joy, and shares the spoil;
Across the fresh turned earth he hops,
Before a luscious worm he stops,
Then chirps, "this farmer's mighty good
To plough all day to find me food."

At noon the plough-boy thunders "whoa,"
A word that well the oxen know,
And one they always will obey,
And they are left to meal and hay;

Meanwhile the farm hands never fail
To empty clean the dinner pail.

Turn, turn, turn, empty are crib and bin,
Turn, turn, turn, ploughing the daisies in,
Turn, turn, turn, breaking the tufted sward,
Turn, turn, turn, reaping a rich reward.

The dinner done they're off again —
These farmers are no idle men —
He earns his bread who tills the soil
By honest sweat and patient toil;
Still up and down with ceaseless tread,
This is the way his babes are fed.

And when the plough-point strikes a rock
And sends it back with sudden shock,
To dig the farmer in the ribs,
He takes fresh hold upon the nibs,
And pulls the plough back into place,
And moves along with cheery face.

Turn, turn, turn, empty are crib and bin,
Turn, turn, turn, ploughing the daisies in,
Turn, turn, turn, breaking the tufted sward,
Turn, turn, turn, reaping a rich reward.

The weary oxen reek with sweat,
The farmer's cotton shirt is wet,
Still up and down he patient goes,
Turning those narrow clean-cut rows,

Turning the furrows one by one
Until the long bright day is done.

Then towards the barn the cattle head
Where they are stalled and groomed and fed.
But still in sleep they hear the cracks
Of Sam's long whip across their backs,
And stir uneasy in their stalls
Until the new milch heifer bawls.

And e'en the farmer old and wise
Oft rises in his bed and cries —
"Whoa! Sam, look out, we've struck a rock!"
And then he hears the kitchen clock
Just striking three, so down he lies
And sleep soon holds his tired eyes.

Turn, turn, turn, empty are crib and bin,
Turn, turn, turn, ploughing the daisies in,
Turn, turn, turn, breaking the tufted sward,
Turn, turn, turn, reaping a rich reward.

BILIN' SAP

You boys all know how in the airly Spring,
Wal, say about the time the bluebird comes,
How 'tis the groun' begins ter thaw an' freeze
Along the sunny slopes beside the woods,

An' how the sap goes creepin' up by day
Inter the limbs an' shoots upon the trees
An' how the cold at night will send it back
Agin a-racin' down into the roots
Ter keep all snug and warm till mornin' comes.
The snow aint gone 'cept here an' there a bit
Upon the hills that look all bare and burnt
Instead o' cold an' kinder lonesome too,
Like some poor robin that yer see in fall
After the rest have gone an' snow has come,
A-hoppin' round upon a leafless limb
Perkin' his feathers up an' makin' b'lieve
That he aint cold an' mighty lonesome too.
It aint so piercin' cold these days except
By spells, but now an' then the rough March
      wind
Gits on a rampage an' careers about
An' howls in at the cracks an' shakes the house
Like he was mad,—That's Winter's dyin' kick.

Wal, jest about this time it gits ter look
Like sugarin', so when the wind gits right
An' it will freeze by night an' thaw by day,
Then boys look out fer jest a rush o' sap;
'Tis then we git the spiles an' buckets out
An' set the camp. I tell you what 'tis fun
This tappin' trees, sendin' the gleamin' bit
Inter the wood, seein' the shavin's creep
Out on the bit an' fall upon the snow

Wet with the life blood of the mighty tree;
An' then ter see the sap come spirtin' out
As bright and sparklin' as the mornin' dew,
An' then ter hear it drop into the pail
As stiddy as an ole-time wooden clock —
A kinder sayin'—drink, drink, drink;
A drop aint much yer say, wal, no. but then
When you've a thousand trees a-tickin' so
You'll find out soon it piles the sap up fast,
An' that's jest what this tale is comin' to.
When sap has been a-runnin' for a week
Right smart, that is it does not run much nights,
The storage tubs an' pans git brimmin' full
An' runnin' over too, 'tis then the boys
Go up ter camp ter bile the sap at night.
But they are used to that 'ere kind o' thing
An' there aint nuthin' they would ruther do.

They git a peck o' apples from the bin,
Some but'nuts an' some chestnuts from up stairs,
An' half a dozen ears of popcorn too,
An' p'raps a dozen eggs to help along,
An' then they start up to the sugar house;
The moon is mebbe three hours high by then
An' jest a-smilin' out her purtiest,
Turnin' the snow to sparklin' diamonds
An' makin' gloomy shadows 'hind the trees.
The sugar house looks cheerfuller than home
With its great fire a-glowin' in the arch,

An' steam a-steamin' out through every crack.
Wal, fust they set ter work ter fill the pan
An' git the fire to goin' good an' hot
An' then they try to have a little fun.
The eggs are dropped inter the hoppin' sap
An' biled, the apples toasted by the coals,
The chestnuts roasted hot, and but'nuts cracked,
An' then they spread some blankets on the floor
Before the glowin' arch where it is warm,
An' set down for a feast an' story tell.

And sech tales as them country boys can tell
Things that they've read out of the garret store
Of books an' papers on a winter's night.
Stories of Injun fightin' on the plains,
An' huntin' grizzlies on the mountain wilds
An' trackin' antelopes across the snow,
With jungle tales an' stories of the east.
An' hand ter hand encounters with the lion,
An' tigers mad with hunger and with wounds,
Of buried treasures in the mountain's side,
An' pirate raids upon the open sea.
An' all the time the fitful firelight gleams
An' dances in the arch, sendin' its glow
Far out inter the gloom, then sinkin' low
Leaves all the scene in dark mysterious shade.

An' ev'ry now and then the howlin' wind
Shrieks in the trees like witches ridin' by,

Or makes the big old maple limbs ter squeak
An' groan, then in some sudden lull the crust
Will crack an' snap like ter the sharp report
O' that dread rifle that the red man bears,
An' owls with hideous hoots fill up the gaps.
An' as each tale grows skeerier than the last
The boys draw nearer to the cheerful fire
An' peer inter the gloom with frightened eyes;
An' so they pass the cold un'arthly night
A-chankin' apples an' a-spinnin' yarns
An' skeerin' one another nigh to death
Until the gleamin' stars begin to fade
An' in the east there comes a yaller streak.
An' then they pour the syrup in a tub,
Then hitch it tight upon the ol' hand sled
An' draw it home jest as the breakin' day
Begins to chase the shadows o'er the snow.

MA'S POSY BEDS

When I come hum from work at noon
As tired as I can be,
There is one mighty purty scene
It does me good ter see,
An' that is mother's posy beds,
A-blushin' fit to kill,
With butterflies and bees around,
A-drinkin' o' their fill.

The air is brimmin' over with
A hundred different scents
That come from the syringa bush
Beside the garden fence
An' rose-bushes an' lilacs tall
That grow along the walk,—
But they aint none o' them so gay
As my ole hollyhock.

Somehow I like the good ole kinds
O' posies full as well,
(Instead o' those with Latin names
That nobody can spell),
Like mirigold an' asterziz
An' caliopsis fair,
An' bleedin' hearts an' arder tongues
An' ferns an' maidenhair.

Once when I'ze down ter Bosten town,
As I wuz goin' past,
I turned inter a posy place
Where everything wuz glass,
An' all the posies looked so pale
As though they'd like ter die,
Jest like them little city waifs,
It made me want ter cry.

I tell yer what, the country is
The place ter make things grow,

No matter what the crap may be,
The city haint no show;
An' as for raisin' human souls
An' givin' them a breath
O' God's free air an' sunlight too,
We beat um all ter death.

SONG OF THE WOODSMAN

I hie me away to the forest old
On a winter's morn when the air is cold
And the white snow gleams in the morning sun
And every twig is a diamond,
The trees are bending beneath the snow
That falls in showers as the cold winds blow,
A heavy load bears the evergreen
And scarce a leaf of the laurel is seen.

With a steady stroke at the tallest oak
The forest ever grows,
I'll lay it low in the gleaming snow
To music of my blows;
Then gaily sing while the woodlands ring
With echoes of the ax,
Though the trees are tall I'll conquer them all
And break their sturdy backs.

I take my stand by the lordly tree
That now hath stood full a century

And raised on high its majestic form
In the Summer breeze and the Winter's storm;
I measure it with a woodman's eye,
Its towering form 'gainst the Winter sky,
And choose the spot where the tree must fall
With a deafening crash, at the woodman's call.

With a steady stroke at the tallest oak
The forest ever grows,
I'll lay it low in the gleaming snow
To music of my blows;
Then gaily sing while the woodlands ring
With echoes of the ax,
Though the trees are tall I'll conquer them all
And break their sturdy backs.

The bright ax gleams as it goes up slow
And then it falls with a ringing blow,
The sharp blade sinks in the tender sap
And falling chips leave a bleeding gap,
And wide and deep grows the woodman's cut
As he hews away at the royal butt,
And one by one through the yearly rings
The bright ax sinks while the woodman sings.

With a steady stroke at the tallest oak
The forest ever grows,
I'll lay it low in the gleaming snow
To music of my blows;

Then gaily sing while the woodlands ring
To echoes of the ax,
Though the trees are tall I'll conquer them all
And break their sturdy backs.

A squirrel starts from his winter hole
Where he keeps house in a hollow bole
And views the stranger with curious eyes,
(And barks and chirps) as the ax he plies;
A snow-bird too from a distant limb
Flies down to take a peep at him,
And waits and chirps till the lunch hour comes,
Then makes a meal on the scattered crumbs.

With a steady stroke at the tallest oak
The forest ever grows,
I'll lay it low in the gleaming snow
To music of my blows;
Then gaily sing while the woodlands ring
To echoes of the ax.
Though the trees are tall I'll conquer them all
And break their sturdy backs.

And soon the woodsman with cautious eye
Will view the top in the steel-blue sky
To see if the tree has begun to lean,
Or if a stir in its twigs are seen;
Then comes a quake through the noble tree,
As though it writhed at its destiny,

And then a creak as the firm wood breaks,
And the monarch falls and the firm earth shakes.

With a steady stroke at the tallest oak
The forest ever grows,
I'll lay it low in the gleaming snow
To music of my blows;
Then gaily sing while the woodlands ring
With echoes of the ax,
Though the trees are tall I'll conquer them all
And break their sturdy backs.

HOW BE YER?

I don't gin much for city ways
O' ginning a handshake,
This taking hold o' people's hands
As though you thought they'd break;
I like to hev 'em grip my hand
Like 'twas an ax or plow,
An' gin my arm a wrench an' say
How be yer anyhow?

A LAW OF NATURE

Yer can't plant cabbage seed and get a tater,
Not in my garden patch, an' that aint Nater,
An' he who goes around a-sowin' evil,
Will reap a crap o' pig-weeds from the devil.

VANITY

When I see a feller round a-blowin'
About how much he knows, a kinder crowin'
Over the saints, and over all creation,
I'm mighty glad he aint o' my relation.

OUR SINS

Our sins are like the weeds we see a-growin'
Down in the medder lot when we're a-mowin',
For if there's one a-noddin' in the clover
There's almost sartin sure to be another.

MISCELLANEOUS POEMS

THE CITY OF THE DEAD

Know you the city of the dead —
    A town of much repute?
Where never a word by day is said,
    And all the clocks are mute.

Where joy ne'er comes, nor any woes,
    And sunlight never streams,
Where from his house no tenant goes
    And all the hours are dreams.

The streets are narrow in this town,
    The houses are not tall,
And they are built so far, far down,
    The turf grows over all.

Only their domes and turrets show
    Above the grasses green,
But all are quite alike below
    Where they are never seen.

And every dweller has his name
    Engraved upon the spire,
A word of praise unto his fame,
    Or charity, that's higher.

And people come to read the words,
    But never stay — alas,
Their only true friends are the birds
    The sunlight and the grass.

With every year a phalanx comes
All without sound of feet,
To swell the countless little homes
Along the darksome street,

And some are rich and some are poor,
And others great or small,
But the grass will grow o'er every door
And cover them one and all.

THE GUERDON OF SONG

'Tis not for wealth I sing my simple lays,
Or e'en for fame or for the critic's praise;
But for the joy of feeling and of living
All that I say, and for the joy of giving.

He who can feel that by his life he feeds
A hungry world and fills another's needs,
E'en though his song may be but idle things
Has known the joy for which the poet sings.

TEARS OF ANGELS

Dark was the night, the cheerless starless night,
But darker were the shadows round my soul,
For hope and faith and strength had perished
all
And now it seemed there was no truth, no right.

But while I slept, my sorrows all took flight
 And in my dreams the heavens opened wide,
 And hosts of angels gathered to my side
And gazed on me with faces wondrous bright,
 While down their cheeks there fell great drops
  like rain,
And each did strive to soothe my trembling fears
 With thoughts of things above the vaulted
  blue.

Then breaking morn illumed the earth again,
 And when I sought to trace the angels' tears,
 Behold the grass and flowers were wet with
  dew.

PAIN'S RECOMPENSE

By life's alternate joy and woe
Our sorrows teach us ere they go,
 The highest, noblest lesson;
That where true manhood strongest grows,
Where love in sweetest fragrance blows,
 There sorrow's dewdrops glisten.

PEBBLES AND SHELLS

THE HEIGHTS AND THE DEPTHS

I would not live upon one changeless plain,
With joy or sorrow evermore to reign;
  As blood is darker on the spotless snow,
  So joy is sweeter in the cup of woe.

GOD'S LOVE

  As tireless as the rivers move
    That water vale and lea,
  So flows the river of God's love
    Unto a shoreless sea.

ANGELS OF EARTH

We think of angels as ethereal things,
With souls as spotless as their shining wings,
But unto some, upon this earth 'tis given
To far transcend the angel hosts of heaven.

HOME

Build man a palace turreted and grand,
Embellish it with gold from India's strand,
Then furnish it voluptuous and fair,
Yet 'tis not home without his love is there.

A FABLE IN ART

Long years ago, in some forgotten reign,
There lived a limner wedded to his art,
With but one purpose burning in his heart;
That by his brush, the dreamland in his brain
Might find a place in galleries of Spain.
And with this purpose glowing in his heart
Before his easel sat he years apart,
Until at last his strength began to wane.
But with the years a wondrous landscape grew
Beneath his brush, so subtle was its hue
Of crimson clouds, no artist could declare
From whence it came, until one morn they
    found
The hand grown cold, above his heart a wound
From whence there flowed the crimson rich and
    rare.

SATISFIED

When in this life a soul shall find
That which shall satisfy the heart and mind
  In all its craving, doubting, hoping, striving,
  Then to that soul is life made worth the living;
And in that hour unto that soul 'tis given,
To know in part the boundless joys of heaven.

THE POET'S JOY

A grain of gold without alloy,
A perfect thing from life's poor alchemy,
Dearer than wealth or fame or power to me
I hold this sweet delight, the poet's joy.
When I can rise above all low annoy
In matchless flight upon the wings of song
And sing a strain so deep, so pure so strong
That all earth's sordid strife cannot destroy
The waking dream, or kill the living thought.
When I can feel in truth that I have wrought
Into the lives and deeds of men to be
A noble thought, that they may know my power
When I am gone; my joy in that brief hour
Is more than years of baser ecstacy.

AMPLIUS

Sweet banished years of joy and youth,
   Of twenty-five this is the last;
I cannot weave its fragile woof,
   That day is done, that die is cast.

I cannot summon childhood days
   And blend them with thy coming years,
Or place its coronet of flowers
   Upon a brow that smiles through tears.

I cannot pierce those distant days
  That ne'er have seen the tide of time
And sing a prophet's wondrous lays,
  I only know a poet's rhyme.

This day God gives thee something grand,
  A life of action and of power,
A throbbing heart, a willing hand,
  A noble art, a fleeting hour.

Let every year that marks thy life
  Be filled with noble actions done,
Let every effort in the strife
  But nerve thee for a greater one.

Fight bravely onward unto death
  And thou shalt yet be known of kings,
Let every heart beat, every breath,
  But lift thee up to higher things;

Then when thou lay'st thine armor down,
  Amid the battle's dust and heat,
Thou shalt receive a golden crown,
  A scepter and a regent's seat.

THE SOUL OF ART

A strange uncertain mass the colors lay,
In wild profusion on the pallette board,
And who would guess that in that mass was
    stored

The matchless glory of an autumn day,
Or who would dream that mortal would essay
To catch the light upon a stream that poured
Down   jagged   cliffs,   where   flaming   maples
    towered,
And autumn's mantle over the fair earth lay.

Yet one I knew took up the lifeless brush
And spread the paint with such consummate skill,
That one could see the sunlight dance and thrill
Along the leaves and hear the torrents rush.
It was not that the sight could understand,
It was the soul that moved the artist's hand.

A HEART OF GOLD

A beggar by the roadside sat him down,
His clothes were poor, he had a heart of gold,
Upon his throne there was a mighty king,
His robes were fair, his heart was hard and cold.
Which would you love, the beggar or the king?
One was a man — the other, well — a thing.

PEBBLES AND SHELLS

THE ANTIPODES

Hate is a dagger in the human heart,
And he who hates will surely feel its smart;
Love is an angel in a woman's eyes
That brings the earthly nearer Paradise.

A LESSON

If e'en one star in heaven fails to shine
The earth is darker for that loss of light;
If thou canst laugh and smile in sorrow's
night,
The earth is brighter for that smile of thine.

PATIENCE

Notice how patiently the spider spins,
Forming his fabric fair by slow degree;
And cannot man, as patiently as he,
Strive on and on and on, until he wins?

HAVE CHARITY

Have charity for all thy fellow men,
Despise not him whom sin hath left alone;
When we shall see and know as we are known,
The darkest soul may prove the fairest then.

GETHSEMANE

Ye proud nobility who walk the earth
   In unconcern, where every form of want,
   Of sin and crime and hunger grim and gaunt
Stand specter-like beside the poor man's hearth,
And rob humanity of joy and mirth,
     Where God's free sunlight never deigns to
     slant
     Across the floor of dens where demons haunt
The human soul — O put aside your birth,
     Your heritage of ease, and for one day
     Come forth with me to life's Gethsemane to
     pray;
Take all this heavy load, the whole world's rue
     Upon yourselves, as Jesus did of old,—
     Then be your hearts like icebergs frigid cold,
They needs must melt with pity through and
     through.

THE HIDDEN LIFE

Deep down beneath the billows' angry sweep,
Beyond the fury of the raging sea,
There is a world of silent mystery;
There coral mountains lift their hoary heads,
Where sea shells lie in glowing amber beds,
And all is wrapped in deep eternal sleep.

Deep down beneath the world's distress and pain
Beyond the fury of life's ceaseless storm,
To noble souls there is eternal calm;
There fancy sits in bright illumined caves
And hoards the treasures of the stormy waves,
Where quiet truth and beauty ever reign.

ASLEEP

WRITTEN FOR OLIVER WENDELL HOLMES

The bard was good, and Death it had no fears,
  So he was waiting but to fall asleep;
  His life had been so full and broad and deep
With all the rich experience of years,
And he had seen so much of pomp and peers
  And stood so high upon achievements steep
  That what was left but just to fall asleep.
They gathered round his bier in grief and tears,
One placed a wreath upon his pulseless breast,
  One kissed the lips that never more would sing,
  Their tears, their flowers and all that love
     could bring
Were proffered him e'er he was laid to rest;
  And while the nations honored him and wept
  The noble bard in sweet oblivion slept.

ALBUM LEAVES

True friends are like the stars in heaven
That ever steadier brighter glow
When all is darkness here below,
For when our sorrows dim the sight
And all about is dark as night,
Their loves and sympathies are given.

True love is like a fragile flower
That smiling opes its tender eyes
And breathes sweet fragrance to the skies,
For though its sphere be great or small
It sheds a beauty over all
And cheers and gladdens every hour.

Kind words are like the gentle rain
That melts away the ice and snow
And bids the happy brooklet flow,
For though the heart be cold and drear,
A kindly word of hope and cheer
May melt away its icy chain.

Good deeds are like the days of spring
That fill the heart with joy and mirth
And draw rich beauties from the earth,
For he who giveth full and free,
Will find his bread upon the sea
Within the kingdom of the king.

LIFE IS A DAY

Life is a day of sun and shower
And none can tell how it will end,
A sunny morn may showers send,
A cloudy dawn will often mend,
But man must upward, onward wend
And do his duty hour by hour.

THE BROKEN HARP

My golden harp lay broken on the floor,
    My shattered hopes among its parted strings—
    Ah who can know the joy of him who sings,
Or grief of him whose heart will sing no more,
'Twas not for me to add unto the store
    Of golden thoughts in sweet pathetic rhyme
    That loftly bards had given to their time—
Not e'en one thought, one little maxim more;
But I had lived to sing a noble strain
    That thought let fall from off a burning pen
    Might raise the souls and touch the lives of
        men.

Long years rolled by, the harp ne'er spoke again,
    But love still labored on through grief and
        wrong
    And made one life a sweet immortal song.

PEBBLES AND SHELLS

THE KING AND THE BEGGAR

A beggar asked for alms beside the palace gate,
The king passed by and left him poor and
  desolate
  But on the morn he was a king beyond the
  skies,
  The king a beggar at the gate of Paradise.

DO ANGELS CARE?

Do angels care for Shakespeare and the rest,
Have they no kindred with the human breast?
  If they care not for all that man has done,
  How can he care for heaven when 'tis won?

LIFE'S ALCHEMY

Into the crucible of grief a life was thrown,
  Awhile the bright flames danced around the
  blackened bowl;
And in the melting heat the liquid metal shone,
  Until the alchemist beheld a spotless soul.

TWO RIDDLES

A little child plays at his mother's knee,
But who can say what man the child will be?
  An aged pilgrim lays life's burden down
  But has he failed, or shall he wear a crown?

THE POET'S ART

How doth the poet weave his magic song,
  His warp the golden threads of living truth,
  With silver words and phrases for the woof,
That all may blend in fabric fair and strong?
He sitteth by his loom and ponders long
    Those things that make or mar the lives of
      men.
From out the depths of all that he has been
He summons back the grief, the strife, the wrong
And lays them all beside the joy of May,
    From every varied hue of mortal strife
    He gathers in each streaming thread of life
And weaves them all into his perfect lay —
    This is the secret of the poet's art,
    Nearer to God, nearer the human heart.

HOMEWARD BOUND

" We're homeward bound," the sailor sings,
" We skim the main with sea-gull wings;
    We care not for the raging storm
    When we can see the mast-head's form,
At Neptune's wrath all sailors laugh
When love is waiting at the wharf.

Above the sacred city on the hill
    Where India's cloudless heavens seem to lower,
And all the earth and air are deathly still,
    There stands dark Dahkma, or the Silent
        Tower.

Deep-lined against the sky its massive form
    Towers heavenward from the place of ceaseless
        prayer,
To front the summer sunshine and the storm,
    And evermore to cast its shadow there.

No voice of gladness stirs its silent sphere,
    And all the place a deathlike stillness keeps,
Save when the vulture screams and hovers near,
    And o'er her love a dark Parseean weeps.

No footfall wakes the chamber of the dead
    Save when a corse is laid upon the floor,
For spirits move with swift and silent tread,
    And Life and Death are parted at the door.

Here side by side is prince and pauper clay,
    And royal ash lies mixed with common dust,
Here pomp and glory vanish with decay
    And selfish man forgets his greed and lust.

Here hoary heads shall lie where babes have slept
    And low degree may mingle in the throng,

Here friends shall sleep with friends that they
     have wept
  And innocence forget its grief and wrong.

And all day long across the tropic plains
    Fair forms are borne by Zerdasht Holy Band,
Up to the hill, in slow and solemn trains,
    While Magi chant the sacred words of Zend.

Out of the orient land the mourner comes
    Bringing the nation's noblest and its best,
Bearing the idols of a thousand homes
    Up to the tower where all at last must rest.

O Dahkma grim! Thou art the bane of life,
    Thy shadows touch the utmost bounds of earth,
And fill man's days with bitterness and strife
    And darken every human life at birth.

But earth and air and sky seem filled with joy,
    Creation smiles and all the world is glad,
In Nature's heart there is no dark alloy,
    Of all her creatures man alone is sad.

Ah no! My soul forgets what Zerdasht saith
    And what the earth and heavens declare to me;
That life is but the highway unto death,
    And death the door to immortality.

THE NOBLEST THING OF ALL

A wondrous thought my idle tongue let fall
  One day while musing o'er the lives of men —
  Of all the noble deeds that e'er have been
Which truly is the noblest of them all?
Was it some deed of arms by Trojan wall,
  Or act of love in some foul prison den,
  Or bold invective from a flaming pen,
Or gentle ministry beside the pall?
  But in the pause my heart made answer bold,
  I knew a life whose days were dark and cold,
Each hour seemed fraught with more than soul
    could stand
  Of bitter grief that turns the heart to stone —
  Yet on that face a smile like heaven shone.
This was the noblest thing of all, 'twas grand!

THE ROAD TO FAME

The road to fame is not up shining stairs
That lead unbroken to the dizzy heights,
But he who climbs must leap from cliff to cliff,
By dangerous ways through weary days and
    nights,
Until he finds a foot-hold in some rift
Or niche of fame, where all the world may see,
Where he can stand and view humanity.

PEBBLES AND SHELLS

THREE SCORE AND TEN

Only a ripple on the sea of time
  As though 'twere stirred by some uncertain
    breath,
Then comes the calm e'er it has space to climb,
  And some poor soul has passed from birth to
    death.

AGE AND YOUTH

When we are young we long for years
  To give us wisdom, strength and truth;
When we are old, with smiles and tears
  We oft recall the joys of youth.

THE DEAD SEA

This dark and lifeless never changing sea
Is like a life that knows not charity.
  It drains the verdant earth but never gives,
  And from that circumstance it never lives.

RICH OR POOR

The rich man sighs for love and sympathy
  And those dear things that ne'er are bought
    or sold;
  The poor man sighs because he has no gold
To build a mansion for his loved ones, three.

THE MIDSHIPMITE

Ah yes my lads, 'was long ago,
   It seems an age to me,
Since good ship Victor spread her sails
   And then put out to sea.

She was as staunch and true a ship
   As ever sailed the main,
She'd hold her own on any sea,
   In wind or hurricane.

And all our crew were stalwart men
   As ever walked a deck,
Our mate had sailed in unknown seas
   And outlived many a wreck.

Our captain was a sailor born
   And well he kept his log,
Yet had one fault, one grievous sin,
   He guzzled too much grog.

But not of these I tell my tale,
   'Tis of the midshipmite,
He was the joy of all the ship
   Our solace and delight.

His eyes were blue as any sea,
   His cheeks were like the dawn,
And fair his shock of flaxen hair
   As wind e'er blew upon.

He was an orphan and a waif,
　Yet happy as a king,
And it was music to my soul
　To hear him laugh and sing.

The winds were fair and all went well
　Until we struck a sea
Along the low Australian coast,
　In latitude twenty-three.

Where not a ripple stirred the brine
　Or e'en a sail would fill,
Where all was brazen overhead
　And all was deathly still.

Three dreary days we sweltered there
　Beneath that sky of brass,
Three weary days we floated there
　Upon that sea of glass.

Then suddenly from out the south
　There grew a tiny speck,
"Haul in your canvas," roared the mate,
　"Or we shall be a wreck!"

Old sailors sprang upon the yards
　And quickly shortened sail,
And in a breath the vessel stood
　Trimmed ready for the gale.

The typhoon struck us full astern,
 Stout masts bent down like reeds,
She rose and fell, then rose again
 To meet old ocean's steeds.

In serried ranks they charged her deck,
 They drenched the scattered crew,
And lower still the mastheads bent
 As still the tempest grew.

But good ship Victor laughed to scorn
 The winds that blew so free,
And raised her crest above the waves
 And bounded o'er the sea.

Then staggering upward from below
 Our drunken captain came,
His bloodshot eyes seemed filled with fire,
 His swarthy cheeks aflame.

" What means this coward crew! " he cried,
 " What! fear you such a gale?
. All hands aloft upon the yards
 And set the topmost sail.

What then my lads, you will not go? "
 The frenzied captain cried,
" I'll teach this crew to disobey —
 Bring out my old rawhide! "

The middy stood bewildered there
  Uncertain what to do,
He saw the captain's sullen glare,
  The darkly frowning crew;

He saw the snow white canvas gleam
  Upon each straining mast,
He heard the beating of his heart
  Above the howling blast.

Then like a hound the captain sprang,
  And forward sprang the mate
To snatch the middy from his grasp —
  Ah God! too late! too late!

He seized him fiercely by the throat —
  My blood ran cold in me,
Then hurled him far across the deck
  Into the raging sea.

A wild, wild cry, like a sea gull's scream,
  Fell sharply on the air,
And a stifled groan from man to man
  Went upward like a prayer.

No boat could live in such a sea,
  No hand but God's could save,
He rose upon the billow's crest,
  Then sank beneath the wave.

A moment more and far away
  I saw him rise and dip,
And when the midshipmite went down
  He beckoned to the ship.

We never saw the lad again
  Or heard his merry song,
And all our hearts were filled with grief
  And all the ship seemed wrong.

But in the watches of the night
  Our wretched captain swore
He heard the middy's cry for help
  Above the deafening roar.

And when the morning came again
  With breeze and balmy air,
He saw his form upon the waves;
  His hand still beckoned there.

Thus wore the weary voyage on
  Until we entered port,
With changing winds and fickle seas
  And all things out of sort.

We lay in port a weary week
  And then put out to sea,
The middy followed in our wake,
  All was adversity.

The winds blew east the winds blew west
  They then blew north and south,
The sea was smooth the sea was rough,
  And it ope'd its yawning mouth.

We shifted sail and tacked and turned
  To please the powers that be,
Until we reached that selfsame coast
  In latitude twenty-three.

And there we hung upon that sea
  As we had done before,
As lifeless as a phantom ship
  Beside a phantom shore.

Then once again there came a speck
  From out the brazen south,
And once again his steeds rose up
  When Neptune blew his breath.

We did not hear the demon come,
  It came with noiseless feet,
Until the sea about the ship
  Was all one boiling sheet.

Until the tempest struck the ship
  And stripped her of her sails,
Until the monsters of the deep
  Were pouring o'er our rails.

We tried to keep her to the wind —
She would not mind her wheel,
The billows tossed her bow about
And made her rock and reel.

Still louder and still louder grew
The tempest's mighty roar,
And all that time our helpless ship
Swept onward toward the shore.

" It is the lad! " our captain cried,
" That stirs this angry sea,
I see his hand above the mast,
It beckons unto me."

We heard the breakers on the shore
Above the howling gale,
And fearless hearts grew cold with fear,
And swarthy cheeks grew pale.

Swift as a mountain avalanche,
Dread messenger of grief,
Our good ship skimmed the rushing seas
And struck upon the reef.

And where she struck the breakers lay
Like snow-fields, but alas!
Beneath their foam were jagged rocks —
Her hull broke up like glass.

Her tall masts fell like broken reeds
  Into the boiling brine,
And hull and bar and canvas lay
  Along the dread snow line.

Half stunned and bleeding, on a spar,
  With knotted ropes made fast,
Made sport of by the cruel waves,
  Derided by the blast,

I tossed upon the angry sea
  Until its wrath was gone,
At morn it left me on the strand,
  Half naked and alone.

I saw the wreck along the shore
  By mighty billows rolled,
I saw her timbers on the sand,
  Amid the slime and mold.

And in the pauses of the blast,
  The breakers seemed to say,
" Vengeance is mine," Jehovah saith,
  " I surely will repay."

PEBBLES AND SHELLS

ONLY A PEBBLE

Only a little pebble on a rocky strand
Roll'd by the restless sea till it shall be but sand;
   Only a little life upon existence's shore
    Tost by the tides of time till it shall be no
     more.

MAN'S LITTLENESS

Man serves his generation and his day,
But time, it stretcheth e'en from aye to aye;
And his great world, where boundless oceans toss,
Is but an atom in the universe.

AN ESTIMATE

In youth we ask if he be sharp of wit,
Or rich, or famed before we call him fit;
   In age we ask if he has suffered long
    And nobly done his part through praise or
     wrong.

THE FAIREST HAND

The fairest hand may not be soft and white,
   Encased in gloves, neat-fitting to the arm;
The hand of toil may be a fairer sight
   When it holds charity within its palm.

A QUERY

If nature feels the thrill of might
In every leaf and blade and flower
That struggles upward toward the light
Obedient to some hidden power;
Why does man grovel in the dust
And foster greed and pride and lust,
Instead of reaching up and striving
Toward a higher, nobler living?

THE STREAM OF LIFE

I stood at morn upon the crowded street
  Where men of every clime and country throng,
Where rich and poor and high and lowly meet,
  And mingle in the tide that sweeps along,
And sought to read upon that troubled sea
  Where righteousness went side by side with
      wrong,
The hopes and fears of all humanity;
  And this became the burden of my song.
Oh! darkly rushing stream, one moment stay,
  And let me linger on life's sunny shore,
  And dip more deeply into hnman lore,
And learn to love and trust and truly weigh
  The things of life ere it shall be no more —
  But still the stream swept onward as before.

BROKEN RAILS

The swift express that never fails
  Sweeps onward to its journey's end,
And wife and child and happy friend
Look forward to the city's pales,
Unconscious of those broken rails.
  A plunge, a crash, no time to slack,
  The swift express has jumped the track,
And shrieks and moans and dying wails,
  And fearful flames with lurid light
  Make hideous the coming night.
No wonder that the brave heart quails
  Along life's dark uncertain track,
  Man knoweth not what hour to slack
Or where to find the broken rails.

TO PADEREWSKI PLAYING

'Tis vain for me to praise thy matchless power
  Strange dweller in a land of mysteries,
  When thou dost lean across the snowy keys
And fill my soul with feeling's richest dower,
Long years of baser life in that sweet hour
  Are awakened by the magic of thy strain,
  When tender love and joy and bitter pain
Sweep o'er my soul, like breezes o'er a flower.

O smite the keys and to my fevered soul
From out thy life let such an anthem roll
That I shall hear and see and understand
The mysteries of life, teach me thy fire
And I will string my poor impassioned lyre
And sing the world an anthem new and grand.

UPON THE HEIGHTS

I stood at evening on the solemn heights,
  Upon the spot where earth and heaven meet,
  I saw the broad earth lying at my feet,
Her bosom set with myriad twinkling lights,
  I heard a church bell tolling sacred rites,
And faint and far a nightbird's plaintive call,
I felt the love that broodeth over all
  And winged my soul to new and higher flights.

It was not night, mine eyes were growing dim,
  I stood upon the hoary heights of years,
  Above the plain of youthful joys and fears
And saw e'en to life's dark horizon rim;
  All things were plain, the darkest clouds were
    riven,
  And hosts of stars illumined the gates of
    heaven.

TRUE RICHES

Man is the mighty arbiter of fate,
   The prince of power, of pleasure and of art;
   From out himself he rules the human heart,
And fills his little world with love or hate.
The poor man stands beside the rich man's gate
   And wonders if a mansion in the skies
   Could give more pleasure to his hungry eyes,
The owner grumbles o'er his broad estate.

   It is not what we have that gives content,
But what we give unto another's need —
The nude we clothe, the hungry that we feed,
   And if we want above what Heaven hath sent.
   The rich man's gold shall make him doubly
      poor
   If beggars turn them hungry from his door.

PEBBLES AND SHELLS

WISDOM

Happy is he who takes life as it seems,
Nor seeks to pierce the vista of his dreams,
  But he who looks for wisdom's priceless dower
  Shall wound his hand upon a thorny flower.

APPEARANCES

A coat of rags oft holds a heart of gold
  And kindliness beyond our estimate;
  While cassimere oft covers up the hate
And pride and vice of hearts unkind and cold.

A DAY IS A STITCH

A day is a stitch in the woof of time
  And if you live it wrong,
'Twill mar all the days of the year that chime
  And make your life less strong.

LOST HOPES

Full many a gallant ship I send to sea
  To battle with the wind and rain;
And some of them come bravely back to me,
  But more are never seen again.

www.ingramcontent.com/pod-product-compliance
Lightning Source LLC
Chambersburg PA
CBHW030125030726

47498CB00007B/2551